This book is dedicated to my children

First published 2012

ISBN   978-1-4716-2745-3

TALES FROM HOCKLEY WOODS

Jenny Titford

Preface

There are many people who never read introductions to books. Instead, they prefer to dive straight into the story and assume they will find out everything they know about the events, characters and places. However, I do hope you are one of those rare people that are just a little bit curious. If you are, and you have come this far, then welcome and please carry on reading just for a page or so.

The stories in this book are all set in a real place and some of the stories are based on real events. It is up to you to decide which stories are true.

The main characters are the children, Lauren and Chris. Lauren is three years older than her brother Chris. They both have blond hair and they are quite tall for their age. Lauren has a pale complexion that used to be called 'English Rose' which sounds rather lovely. She has stormy-grey coloured eyes with flecks of green and blue, an upturned small nose and just a few freckles. She has a few strands of red hair at the back of her head: a small clue that her mother has red hair. Lauren is one of those girls that are annoyingly good at everything they do and she was born with a wonderful singing voice. She is also incredibly kind, thoughtful, imaginative and inclined to be a bit dramatic.

Chris is a quieter person altogether. He is more of a thinker than a doer and he reads books that are really meant for adults. He questions everything and always has to know why things are the way they are. This makes him a good mathematician and he will probably be an excellent scientist one day. He has startlingly blue eyes that twinkle with amusement at all the antics of his family. He too has freckles but he has the sort of skin that goes golden in the summer so he is able to stay out in the sun longer than his older sister. Chris is also a very giving person who remains loyal and true to those he cares about.

Another character that you will meet is their sister Faye who is nine years older than Lauren. Faye is a collector of waifs and strays and frequently finds sick animals to tend to and keep safe from harm. She has a natural affinity with small creatures and has many of her own tales to tell and we may well have to write another book for her one day.

So there you have it, except I forgot to tell you about me. Well, I'm Mum and as well as my own three children I have been a mother to three step-children and two orphaned boys who were being brought up by their grandfather, a family friend. They used to come and stay with us in school holidays. Our house was always full of children, friends and assorted pets over the years. The only way I could settle all these young people down at bedtime was by telling them a story and so here is a small collection for you to enjoy.

I would like to give special thanks to my wonderful family for providing the inspiration for the stories that I conjured up at bedtime and on those magical nights every August when we sat out on the flat roof waiting for the shooting stars.

Thank you too for the support I have received from my best friend and husband Les, who believed in me and painstakingly proof read the first few drafts.

Acknowledgements go to Lawrence Cantle who first told us a story of a tramp in London who provided the basis of 'Old Smeller.'

Credit for photo featured in 'The Demented Squirrel,' Ed Sweeney.

Contents

The Demented Squirrel

There is a legend, that deep in the heart of Hockley Woods, in an area where families often get lost, a disturbing creature can be found.

Many have wondered about the strange goings on in the trees and hidden pathways and many rumours have spread like 'Chinese Whispers' – each retelling of the story becoming more and more fanciful.

Many, many years ago, probably before you were born, the woods were a peaceful place with very few visitors. Nowadays there are clearly signposted routes you can take but away from these you will find the dark, secret woodland places where shy creatures hide away from humans. You may also notice that there are raised walls made of earth and these mark ancient boundaries that were built when people came to let their pigs graze and snuffle around for delicacies.

It is in one of these secret areas, about five minutes away from the main path that our furry fiend has built up his fearsome reputation. Notice I said fiend not friend – that was not a spelling mistake!

Unwary explorers who venture here usually run back to the safety of the marked paths with cries of alarm and shouts to others not to go in there! The reason for all this panic is quite simply a tiny chap intent on deterring humans – especially children. He is very, very old and very, very grumpy. This particular creature is a grey squirrel that sits high in the treetops and bombards the person below with anything that comes to paw but mostly he throws acorns he has secreted in tree trunk stores. He loves to strike in the summer months when nobody can see him behind all the leaves and his acorns are as hard as can be because they have dried out from the previous autumn.

Imagine taking a nice stroll in the summer sunshine and suddenly finding things falling on your head. It is very alarming indeed!

I first encountered our strange squirrel on a summer walk with my children, Lauren and Christopher and our dogs, Merlin and Pebble. Merlin was a very special, blue-merle Border collie and

Pebble was a smaller than average English Pointer. Pebble was the runt of her litter and that means she was the smallest puppy who could not fend for herself and had to be helped to get milk from her mum when all her brothers and sisters pushed her out.

We were walking along one of our favourite routes when Pebble dashed into the undergrowth chasing something she had sniffed out and Merlin dashed after her. Next thing we knew, they were running back towards us with yelps and barks! We wondered what had spooked them and were a bit nervous because it was dark and overgrown and we didn't really want to go and explore. We did not give it much more thought and carried on with our walk.

The dogs reacted the same way on a number of occasions through the summer months but we were really too afraid to investigate. Then autumn came and it was time to go and collect chestnuts that were abundant in this part of the woods. It turned out to be our first, personal encounter with the squirrel. We were busy looking amongst all the fallen leaves looking for the fattest chestnuts which we were all collecting in our carrier bags and we wandered off the path in every direction with cries of delight whenever we found an area with lots and lots of nuts.

Suddenly, Christopher shouted out, 'What's that? Ouch!'

I called out not to be so silly, it was just more chestnuts dropping off the trees but he called out again, 'Mum, something is throwing nuts at me!'

I said, 'Don't be so silly, Chris. I expect the wind is blowing them down.'

However, I did walk over to where he was standing and then I too felt something bounce off my head and then another, and another! Large chestnuts were falling on our heads but nowhere else. It was quite painful because they were still in their spiky shells and very heavy. We looked up warily to see what was causing this unexpected windfall. There was hardly a breeze and the treetops were quite still.

Then, pointing upwards, Chris shouted, 'Look Mum, there's a squirrel dislodging nuts!'

By this time, Lauren had joined us and she looked up into the trees only to have a chestnut land on her forehead. 'Ow, that really hurt! What is that squirrel doing?'

Then both Lauren and Chris yelled, 'Let's get out of here, that squirrel is mad!'

We all ran out of the glade onto the path and laughed and all spoke at once,

'What on earth was that all about?'

'I'm sure it was doing it on purpose.'

'That really hurt.'

'Have I got a mark on my head?'

I told them it was highly unlikely that any squirrel would have any intention of doing something on purpose and it was probably just running along the branch above looking for nuts for his winter store. However, even I had my doubts because it did appear to be quite a ferocious attack. We crept back into the glade, looking warily upwards to see if we could spot him again. Then, once more, chestnuts came crashing down on us along with some acorns and, even worse, a disused bird's nest.

We shrieked and laughed and this seemed to make the squirrel angry because he scurried from branch to branch looking for ammunition. By now, all the branches above us were bare and there was nothing left to throw so the squirrel just sat in one spot and glared at us. I am not sure how a squirrel glares, but he certainly looked really annoyed. We all wondered what he was upset about and tried a few coaxing whistles and chirrups to see if we could make him feel at ease. He ignored us completely and finally sloped off deeper into the woods.

We all wondered what lay behind the attack and came up with a few theories and funny stories.

'I think he doesn't like humans going into his territory,' Chris said. 'After all, it is his home really.'

Lauren liked this idea and we all decided to go back there the next day and see if we could spot him again. We all assumed it was a male squirrel, which was silly really: it could have been a lady squirrel after all. Somehow, we just knew it was bigger and stronger and must be a man squirrel. We walked home with all our chestnuts and I lit the fire ready to do some roasting. We sat down to enjoy our free feast with mugs of hot chocolate and whipped cream and talked a bit more about what had happened.

'I feel sorry for him. He must be very upset about something,' Lauren said.

Chris ate his ninth hot chestnut and waited until his mouth wasn't full and replied, 'I wonder if anyone else knows about this squirrel around here? Maybe we should ask someone?'

I said that was a brilliant idea and that I would go to the office in the main car park of Hockley Woods to see if anyone knew about it in the morning. With that, it was time for baths and bed and bedtime stories, which Lauren and Chris loved so much.

The next day was a school day so I took the dogs for a walk on my own. As usual, the dogs were off like a shot and loving the freedom of not having to be on a lead. It was dog heaven in the woods with so many smells and so many things to chase. We wandered up to the office and luckily found someone very quickly to chat to. He was busy loading up his lorry with logs to take to homes in the area and was glad of a rest and to talk to me. I told him about what had happened and he smiled which made me think he didn't believe me but instead he nodded and murmured, 'Yes, yes,' every now and then.

He said I should talk to someone who knew all about the woods and the stories that had been passed down through the generations and said he had heard about a strange squirrel before. He gave me a telephone number to call and was very mysterious about it. 'This is the number for Mrs Tippett who used to live in an old hovel in the very middle of the woods back in the thirties. You may need to call a few times though, I think she's a bit hard of hearing.'

I thanked him and took the piece of paper away with me wondering whether I should call this woman or not. I thought she might be a bit strange or even a bit creepy. I didn't do anything about it until later in the day when I talked it over with the family. They thought there was no harm in a telephone call and, besides, she might be really interesting.

So, later that evening, I took the plunge and called the number. A quiet and well-spoken voice answered brightly, 'Hello, can I help you?'

I introduced myself and told her why I was calling and who had given me her number and she asked me what I had seen. I told her about all the things that had happened. To my surprise, she laughed so loud and you could tell she knew exactly what I was talking about. She said, 'Oh that's the Demented Squirrel, that is. He's been tormenting people for nigh on seventy years now.'

I said, 'No that can't be, squirrels don't live very long. It must be another squirrel that's picked up this strange behaviour.'

'Oh no, that's definitely the poor creature that I know and love. He's such a poor thing you know - such a sad tale to tell.'

By now, Lauren and Chris had picked up on what was being said and were clamouring around me trying to find out more.

'What's she saying, Mum?' Chris asked, tugging on my arm.

'Does she know about it?' Lauren asked.

'Shh, give me a minute and I'll find out,' I whispered back.

Mrs Tippett was still talking to me and I missed what she had said but it sounded like, 'Do you want to come over for a cup of tea sometime?'

'Yes, that would be lovely,' I replied (thinking I must be mad). 'When is a good time for you?'

We agreed to meet up in a few days' time as she had lots of blackberry jam to make and elderberry wine to bottle. I did wonder what I had got myself into. She then said, 'And please do bring your children, I would love to meet them. How old are they?'

I replied that Lauren was ten and Chris was seven and was it all right and wouldn't she find it tiring? To which she laughingly replied, 'Goodness no, I love children. They have such open minds and wonderful imaginations.'

So it was all confirmed and although I felt a bit nervous about going to a stranger's house with my young children, I thought that a woman of such a considerable age wouldn't pose any threat. The children may have great imaginations, but so do I and I pictured us sipping her elderberry wine and getting very drowsy like Lucy in Mr Tumnus' house in Narnia. (If you haven't read 'The Lion, The Witch and the Wardrobe' then I really recommend you do). Just in case, I asked my husband to drop us off at her house and pick us up after an hour, to be safe.

All this caution was unnecessary though, because when we arrived there later in the week after school, we had the warmest welcome ever. A woman with the sweetest face and twinkly blue eyes you could ever wish for in a grandmother ushered us in. She was quite tall for someone so old and stood very straight. Her silvery hair was swept up in a French pleat and she wore Levi jeans with a soft blue, check shirt. She sounded quite posh and you suspected that she would offer us tea and scones and pronounce them scon not scone!

'Come in, come in and make yourselves at home. You can sit wherever you feel comfortable – on the floor, in the window seat – whatever you feel cosy in. Now what would you like? Tea? Milk? A cold drink?'

We all said thank you: I said I would like tea and the children asked for cold drinks. She came over with one of those lovely cake stands that you only get in shops and on it there were flapjacks, fairy cakes and home-made shortbread. Our mouths were watering! She gave us all tiny plates to use and proper napkins so we knew we were all expected to be on our best behaviour. When we were all settled, she spoke.

'Well, your mother has been telling me about a certain squirrel that has been throwing things at you and I have to tell you, I know this old gentleman very well.'

All our eyes were fixed on her as she began her tale and I am sure our mouths were open too, which is very rude but understandable when you hear what she had to say. Here is her tale:

'A long time ago, when I was just a young girl, I lived in a tiny dwelling in Beech Wood which is the west part of what is now known as Hockley Woods. In those days, there were different woodlands with different names and this area was the quietest. Because I lived so far away from any other houses, it was very peaceful and beautiful and I loved being able to observe all the animals that were normally so shy. It was very near an ancient badger sett and I think they were my favourite creatures of all.

Sometimes, people would come exploring this area with their dogs or on their horses and they were always very careful not to disturb anything or do any damage. However, there was one lad who changed all of this and the inhabitants of the forest will never forget him. This boy was an unhappy chap who was orphaned at the age of six. His father was a soldier who lost his life on the front line and his mother was a nurse who died a few years later from tuberculosis.

After he lost his parents, his aunt took him in but she was a hard, cold woman with no children of her own and not much idea of what a boy needs. It is such a cruel world sometimes and it wasn't the boy's fault but she beat him with a stick whenever he answered her back or if he was only a few minutes late coming back from an errand. This made the boy bitter and angry at the world and I am sorry to say, he took it out on harmless creatures. It started with stamping on ants and grew steadily worse.'

At this point she paused for a sip of tea and said, 'I am sorry if this is upsetting you but this is what happens when there is no love in someone's life.' We all nodded and thought about how lucky we were.

Her story continued.

'One day, while walking in the woods, the boy thought he would have some fun firing stones out of his catapult at our furry friends. It was a wonderful, warm spring day and there were so many newborn animals to be found and for him to torment.

It sounds so cruel but I don't think he valued life much.

Anyway, some of the animals this terrible boy hunted were squirrels. The leaves on the trees were not fully open which made them an easy target. He took aim and missed so many times it was hopeful that no one would get hurt but then, suddenly and tragically, one of his stones hit its mark and he knocked a squirrel off a tree trunk.

He ran over to see what had happened to it and found it lying unconscious in the dried, brown leaves. He kicked it with his foot and turned it over to see if it was breathing but suddenly felt something land on his back and pull at his hair. Crying out and trying to fend this thing off, he flailed his arms around behind his head and ran around in circles screaming. A squirrel was fiercely gripping his hair and scratching his scalp. Its claws were making long, red raw scratches around the boy's neck but he could not get it to let go. He cried out and shouted for help and I must admit I could see what was going on from the end of my little garden but I didn't lift a finger to help him. I was full of admiration for the brave little squirrel. Eventually, the squirrel let go and ran back up into the tree and the boy ran home, no doubt to get another beating from his mean aunt.

I ran out to where the injured squirrel lay and gently picked her up in my apron. I looked up into the treetops and said, 'I will see what I can do to help her.' There was no reply of course as squirrels don't talk do they? I took her indoors and saw that there was little hope and that she was still lying, inert, with her eyes closed. I said a little prayer for her and sat by her side until she stopped breathing. It was very late in the afternoon and deathly quiet as if all the animals knew something was wrong. My tears dropped on to her fur and I wrapped her in one of my nice silk scarves and carried her back to the tree she fell from. I could sense I was being watched so I quietly left her there and hoped they would see that I cared even though other humans didn't.'

Mrs Tippett carried on with her story and we all helped ourselves to some more tea and cakes. Although it was quite sad we were eager to hear what happened next.

'The next morning I walked down to the tree to see if the poor squirrel was still there and to retrieve my scarf. Strangely, she had disappeared and so had my scarf. I wondered if someone had taken it but not many people walked there in the evenings or at night. There was a movement in the branch above so I looked up and there, believe it or not, was my scarf in a nest of twigs and moss! I sat down and waited in silence to see if I could spot anything. Next thing I knew, a large squirrel and a tiny squirrel were above my head and things were dropping on me. I looked up only to be half blinded by an acorn landing in my eye! These two little troublemakers were intent on seeing me off with a bombardment of acorns, twigs and not very dangerous moss. I realised then that this was the mate of the squirrel that had been killed yesterday and the other squirrel must have been their son. I quickly beat a hasty retreat but continued to keep a watch on their nest from then on.

You will not be surprised to learn that this strange behaviour has continued to this day with every generation of this squirrel family being taught to punish us humans for what happened that day. There is a legend that it is the very same squirrel that has lived for over seventy years or that it is the ghost of that poor chap haunting the woods forever. You can believe what you want but that is the tale of this poor, demented creature.'

Mrs Tippett looked at us with amused eyes and we were not sure if she was pulling our legs but she sat back in her chair with a smile and said, 'Well, I have not told that tale for many years but maybe you'll remember it for me and pass it on to your children one day.' She said this looking pointedly at Lauren and Chris who were still agog and not quite believing.

I spoke for them and broke the spell. 'That's an incredible story and I am so glad you told it to us, aren't we glad children?'

Lauren and Chris nodded, struck dumb.

I said, 'Mrs Tippett, thank you so much for telling us about that poor squirrel and his family. It's an amazing tale and I am sure we will never forget it. Thank you.'

'Oh it's nothing dear. I'm glad to remember it at all at my age, that's why I would like you to hear some more stories another day if you want?'

'Oh yes please!' cried Lauren, 'We'd love to hear some more stories.'

'Thank you very much,' said Chris shyly.

'There, that's settled then. You must ask your mummy if you can come back another time and I shall tell you all about the things I have seen in my long, old life. You have been such good children and you have listened so politely. You'd better have another cake as a reward.'

The children needed no encouragement and after another cup of tea and promises to come back we heard a knock on the door and realised that Dad had come back to pick us up. We were quite sad to go and I promised we would call her soon. As we left, Mrs Tippett pressed a jar of home-made jam into my hands and said, 'I really hope we will be friends.' It was a lovely moment.

On the way home and after we were indoors, the children didn't stop talking about the Demented Squirrel until Dad said, 'Please, please stop. I think *I* am going to be demented by all your endless chatter!' At which point the children bundled on top of him and there were cries and squeals and much tickling and stern orders from me to get ready for bed.

Remembrance Valley

Sometimes, in the middle of summer, there comes a day that is cool and misty. No one really knows why this happens and I am sure the meteorologists amongst you will have a scientific explanation. The day before may have been showery and the day after will be very warm, so this is one of those in-between days when you are not sure what to do or where to go.

Should one of these days occur during the summer holidays then you know the children are going to start whining.

'I'm bored.'

'There's nothing to do.'

'Can we go to ....'

You can fill in the dotted line there with anything you know that will be an expensive outing that never quite satisfies a child and leaves everyone feeling a bit flat.

It is on such days that we all need an adventure; so with a bit of planning and foresight you can make the day memorable and exciting despite the weather.

It was on one of those days when I suggested that we all go out for a bike ride round the woods.

'But it's so gloomy,' protested Lauren.

'And cold,' answered Chris.

The dogs, Merlin and Pebble looked up excitedly with their tails wagging because they had hear the word 'Out' and that meant 'Walkies!'

With a bit of persuasion and promises of a return to tea and crumpets, the children agreed and started getting their old clothes on and filling up their drink bottles. I packed some goodies in my rucksack as I knew them both so well and that halfway through our ride they would start getting hungry. Then Dad put his head round the door and said, 'Hang on, I think I'll come with you.'

That was all the persuasion they required, as it wasn't often that their father left his studio to have some time off. However, they did know that it was going to be a while before they could start their journey because Dad was famous for taking ages to get ready!

Soon all the bikes were prepared: the tyres were pumped up, the water bottles put in place, crash helmets were adjusted and cycle gloves put on. The dogs were getting very impatient and kept running under our feet and round in circles. Then we were off dashing down into the woods with Pebble and Merlin running ahead of us. Pebble was always out in front as she was a hunting dog but Merlin was younger than her and he soon caught up. All four bikes came whooshing behind them down their favourite path that wound round to the middle of the woods.

At the first stop to catch our breath, I suggested doing some exploring into an area we had only skirted before. The kids loved this idea as it always meant 'an adventure.' We started climbing up a very steep hill on the far side of the woods and then I led us off to the right into an area where there were no paths at all apart from narrow fox runs. We soon found ourselves in a very dark, quiet landscape full of fallen trees and very little foliage. We must have all felt a bit strange because nobody said a word as we dismounted and negotiated our way around the huge dead tree trunks. Many of them had fallen down with all their roots attached as though giants had ripped them out of the ground. It began to feel very eerie and the air was thick with tension.

'I don't like this place,' whispered Chris.

'Can we get out of here now?' Lauren said, tugging on my sleeve.

Dad was a little way in front of us and looked back saying, 'Come over here, there's something really unusual.'

We had to keep carrying our bikes over all the debris to get to him, which made the children huff and puff with annoyance, but we soon reached him and followed his pointing finger to a beautiful sight. A little way ahead was an area that was just as full of fallen trees but here there were hundreds of thin young trees as far as the eye could see. As we stood there, a shaft of sunlight pierced through the gloom and lit up the new life before us. We just stood there, holding our bikes, and gazing at the scene. Butterflies responded to the warmth and flew out of their various hiding places and danced around in the shifting rays.

Behind us we saw that it was still dark and all around the circle of brilliant sunshine the fallen giants were still sleeping. It was quite hard to tear our gaze away but I think we all wanted to get out into the open air so I suggested we turn left up the hill towards to the fields that encircle Hockley Woods.

It was an enormous relief to be away from the claustrophobic atmosphere of the dark valley and we all sat down on the grass to have a drink and some biscuits from my secret rucksack store. Pebble and Merlin flopped down with steaming bodies from where they had been running so much and I put down their travel bowl with some water to refresh them. They kept pushing each other out of the way to get to it, which made the children laugh.

'What was that place?' Lauren asked.

'It was really spooky,' Chris added.

'I bet there were ghosts there,' Lauren said, trying to scare her younger brother. However, Chris didn't scare that easily and he just pushed her and said, 'Don't be silly, there's no such thing as ghosts.'

'No, of course there aren't any ghosts but I think I know what happened there,' I said. 'Those trees must have been hit by the Great Storm of 1987.'

'What was that Mum?' Chris asked.

'Was that the hurricane? I think I heard about that in school once.' Lauren suggested.

'Yes, it was. It was really bad here but nowhere as bad as it was down on the south coast. I remember it really well and I've got a book about it back at home.'

'I remember sleeping right through it,' laughed Dad. 'I wondered why all the power was down the next day and then your mother told me how she'd been up all night watching the sparks from the pylons.'

'Why did they spark?' asked Chris.

'Because the wind blew so hard the power lines knocked against each other and the electricity in them made flashes a bit like lightning does – it's called arcing. Well, that's the easiest way I can put it for you to understand,' said Dad, looking at me with a look in his eye that said, 'Why does Chris always ask such difficult questions?'

I smiled back: we always laughingly mimicked Chris by all saying 'Why?' whenever he asked questions like 'Why is a bass guitar so big?' to 'Why does the water come out so hot from the tap?' He obviously has an enquiring mind.

I carried on my story while we looked at the view and watched the sun try to burn off the mist in the valley below us. We were already feeling warmer and happier.

'Well that day, or night I should say, of 16th October: it was in the early hours that it struck us. I was woken up by the sound of the wind. I have never heard anything like it. It was absolutely non-stop howling and moaning and really scary. I remembered that before I went to bed that night, I had tapped the barometer like I always did and noticed it was incredibly low. I think it was the lowest I had ever seen it but there was nothing about it on the weather forecast so I didn't think too much of it.

'What's a barometer Mum?' Chris asked.

'Oh, it's a scientific instrument for measuring the air pressure. The weathermen sometimes mention it when they say an area of low pressure is heading for Britain. That usually means rain and wind. If they say high pressure, it often means it will be sunny in the summer. The lower the pressure, the more likely it is that it will be stormy like it was that time.'

'Do you remember how Michael Fish, the weatherman, was teased about his forecast for ages afterwards,' remarked Dad. 'He said that there were going to be high winds but not over England! Poor bloke certainly suffered for that one,' he laughed.

'Yes, I remember. Now they make a fuss if there is simply a gale coming, in case they get the blame again.

'Anyway, going back to the storm, we were living in Rayleigh then and our house looked south west towards Rawreth Lane and that's where I could see all the flashes from the electricity pylons. I knew our power would be cut off. However, the big trees in our back garden were literally bent double and I was amazed they didn't break. Then I saw tiles coming off the roof of the house opposite us and there was a massive crashing sound from further down the road. I think their chimney was blown down. Three of our fence panels blew out and ended up next door and the wind just didn't stop wailing and blowing. I was quite frightened I must admit and went back to bed to feel safe.

The next day we wandered down our road and took in all the damage. A massive old oak tree had fallen across the road and there were roof tiles, fence panels, bricks, upturned wheelie bins and branches everywhere. Your big sisters' schools were closed for the day so we went for a drive down to the coast where it was even worse with whole roofs ripped off buildings, boats up on the road and demolished beach huts. It was amazing.

We then had one of the worst winters too with snow so deep I had to help your big sister with her paper round using a sledge! What a year that was!'

I paused for a drink and then observed that all the fallen trees in the woods must have been from the hurricane and then remembered that there was another storm after we moved to Hockley.

'Yes, it was in January, and Lauren was born by then. She must have been about 2 years old. That was even scarier because it happened in the afternoon and I had to run out to fetch your big sister Faye from school. I remember dodging falling branches and literally having to fight against the wind to walk to the school gates. It was so funny because I was holding your hand, Lauren, and you literally took off like a kite because the wind knocked you off your feet!

We got back home and watched the storm rip through the forest like a wild beast. The noise was absolutely deafening as it was hurtling through all the trees that had no leaves on them because it was January and so it whirred and screamed past the bare branches. It was like watching the sea from our upstairs window. All the treetops were bending one way and then another like wild waves. We lost about four trees from our own garden but thankfully nothing fell on our house. I think that storm was worse because it was during the day and so some people were killed.

Both these storms knocked down millions of trees and some places were very badly hit. Whenever we drove down to Brighton to see your grandparents, we saw whole forests lying flat. It was very sad.'

'Do you think our trees are very sad?' asked Chris.

'Yes, I am sure they are,' I replied.

'What happens to trees when they die?' asked Chris.

'Well..... most of the time, new trees grow up from them when they have fallen over,' I offered hopefully. 'That's what we saw back there.'

'Do trees get ill?' he persevered.

'Yes, they do,' answered Dad. 'That's what happened to all the elm trees in England. They got a nasty disease that killed nearly all of them.'

'Isn't there medicine for them?' Chris continued.

'Don't be daft, they haven't got mouths for medicine,' laughed Lauren.

Chris gave her a shove and crossed his arms sulkily, which made her laugh even more.

'I think they can treat some things but more often than not, they have to destroy diseased trees before it spreads to more.' I explained. 'Maybe we can go back through that route on the way home and take a closer look now that the sun is out. Besides, it's getting quite hot here now.'

'Okay,' they both agreed.

'Yes, I need to get some work done,' said Dad, looking at his watch.

We picked up our bikes and headed back into the woods, which seemed very dark after being out in the sunshine. We had to retrace our path back into the forgotten part of the forest carefully because it was so littered with brambles and branches. The place was much lighter now and looked like a devastated area of fallen dinosaur bones. You could almost imagine a tree trunk being a Diplodocus' backbone! Again, we felt over-awed by the silence of the place and stood in wonder. You could hear a whisper of a breeze soughing gently through the fresh, green saplings and the sunlight glittered on wild flowers and dewy spider webs. The valley had been transformed from a dark, forbidding graveyard into a wondrous, magical tree nursery full of new life. You could almost hear the gentle voices of the soft new leaves soothing the old, slumbering giants on the forest floor, telling them bedtime stories to ease their sorrow.

I looked sideways at Lauren because I could see tears in her eyes and I put my arms around her shoulders. 'It is very sad isn't it? But so beautiful too.'

Lauren sniffed and sighed and leant into me for comfort. Suddenly, before our very eyes, we saw a large fox coming out of a pile of twigs and leaves followed by two tiny baby foxes. They all stopped and stared at us and didn't move or appear to be frightened. We all stared back, hardly daring to breathe. The vixen put her nose up into the air and obviously scented the dogs as well but seemed quite unperturbed by our presence. She merely walked in the other direction at a relaxed pace with her two little kittens behind her. Pebble barked with a low voice.

'Oh they were so sweet,' exclaimed Christopher.

'Yes, they were, weren't they,' I replied. 'Come on then, time to get home.'

Later that night, as they were climbing into bed, Lauren and Chris asked for a story and as always I obliged, using some of the day's events to spur my imagination. I told them the story of the Great Storm and the Burn's Day Storm and how it had such a devastating effect on all the trees in Hockley Woods and all the animals that lived there.

'Normally, when trees get old and finally lie down to rest, the rest of the forest grows up around them and their branches arch over them and protect them because they never truly die, they just pour their life back into the earth. New life springs from their aged bodies and all kinds of animals make their homes in their branches and trunks. The spirits of the trees watch over all these creatures and shelter them from harm.

The woods are full of tree spirits and you can sense them as you walk through the quiet fox paths and secret corners. They are there, quietly whispering to each other and you can feel the softest of touches as you move among them. Some of them are as old as the earth itself and some are young and restless. Some of the trees are coppiced and are bursting with life as new growth emerges from the original tree that was cut down by the woodsmen.

They are the gentlest of all the magical beings in the forest and they sing such sweet songs about youthful bright green leaves and new life and the drawing-in days when their leaves fall and they give us all their wonderful fruit. They sing about the beginning of time and the first life on earth and all the things they have seen through countless centuries.

They are amongst the oldest known living things and they are also the wisest. They have watched dinosaurs and humans and know that they will outlive us all. They understand that life is wonderful and beautiful and needs to be protected. They know that they keep our planet in perfect balance and keep our climate stable. They know that we have to use them to provide warmth and housing but pray we will always remember to replace what we take.

The tree spirits love us and care for us and it is up to us to care for them.'

I could have gone on telling Lauren and Chris about the trees but I could see they were both asleep so I crept from their bedroom and gazed out of the window. A beautiful moon was rising above the treetops and its faint light was reflecting back from the millions of leaves. They shimmered as a breeze blew across and danced in the silvery hue and I was sure I heard them say, 'Yes, we were listening and it was lovely to hear you talk about us. Thank you for visiting our Valley of Remembrance today and please come back one day. So few humans stop to think about us and we wish there were more like you. We are all watching over you and your house. God bless and sleep tight.'

Or was that just my imagination?

Old Smeller

The telephone rang soon after breakfast and it was Mrs Tippett on the other end.

'I'm sorry if it's a bit early but I wondered if the children would like to come and visit today. It's so lovely I thought we could sit in the garden and they could feed the fish.'

'Oh Mrs Tippett, how nice to hear from you,' I replied. 'I'm sure they would love to come over, it's really kind of you to ask. What time would you like us?'

'I think three o'clock would be a good time, if that's all right with you,' she offered.

'All right, we'll see you later, we look forward to it.'

I put the phone down and called Lauren and Chris to tell them where we were going later and they both looked pleased. So using this to my advantage, I suggested they tidy their room before going out. You can imagine their reaction. It never ceases to amaze me how much mess two children can make in such a short space of time and then they expect someone else to put it all back for them. I am sure any mums and dads reading this will be agreeing with me at this point and looking over the top of the book at their own children pointedly.

With much sighing and dragging of heels they went to their room and lazily picked up a couple of things from the floor. I could hear them moaning, 'Why do we have to do housework?' That was from Chris of course – the usual 'Why?'

'I hate clearing up – it's so unfair.' Lauren wailed.

I put my head around the door and glared at them and said I didn't see why I should have to clear up after them as I had enough work of my own to do and Dad was busy in his studio so could they please keep it quiet.

'Also, if you don't clear this mess up we will end up with much worse. Look at those half eaten biscuits and sweets. Pick them up at once or they will go mouldy and then it will start to get very smelly. In fact, I am sure I detect the aroma of sweaty socks in here so they can go in the laundry bin NOW.' I stomped out for good effect and left them to it.

I could hear Lauren chanting, 'Smelly socks, smelly socks, Christopher's got smelly socks,' and Chris shouting back, 'I don't have smelly socks, shut up.'

They were getting fractious and irritable so I was glad we were going out later that day.

The afternoon could not come quickly enough as it had been one of those days when the children were beginning to get on my nerves and I must admit I was not in the best of moods as we set off and warned them both to be good at Mrs Tippett's house. They both sat sulking in the back seat because I had forced them to sit there together to stop the argument about who could sit in the front.

When we arrived at Mrs Tippett's the children soon brightened up with the prospect of fizzy drinks and cake in the back garden. We walked through the house and out through her patio door to find a big parasol up on the lawn and a table full of upside down umbrella food covers that were decorated with ladybirds and strawberries. It looked utterly enchanting and even I started to smile and feel quite pampered. I flopped down in the garden chair while the kids fought over who was going to feed the fish but Mrs Tippett took over for me and intervened.

'Now then children, this is not exactly good behaviour, is it?' she remonstrated with them. 'Let's take turns and you can both put in just a pinch of fish food each.'

So saying, she poured out a small quantity of fish flakes into the lid of the pot and handed it to Chris. He threw it onto the water and watched with glee as the fish greedily sucked the food in. The flakes soon disappeared so Lauren was also then given a chance to throw some food in. This time they took a bit longer to finish their food giving the children an opportunity to watch them for longer before they dived down into the bottom to keep cool.

Mrs Tippett then showed them how to rest their fingertips lightly on the surface of the pond as if they were bits of bread and they shrieked with delight when the fish came and nibbled at them.

'They're tickling me!' Lauren shouted.

'Mum, come and try it,' called Chris.

So I went over and sat on the edge of the pond and did the same and it was amusing to see how the biggest of the Koi carp came and nuzzled at our fingers thinking they were something to eat. It was very funny.

'Thank you so much Mrs Tippett, this is just what the doctor ordered,' I said.

'Why's that? Have you had a hard day?' she replied.

'Yes, the children have been argumentative and difficult today so this was a welcome diversion.'

'Oh dear, what you have you two been quarrelling about then?' she asked Lauren and Chris.

They both spoke at once and kept interrupting each other.

'Chris made all the mess.'

'Lauren kept bossing me about.'

'It was his smelly socks that made our room horrible.'

'No it wasn't, it was all your half eaten packed lunches we found in the wardrobe'

'Shut-up Chris, it wasn't even mouldy.'

'Now then, now then, you two, that's enough arguing. I have a story to tell you about how things can get really bad if you don't keep tidy and clean.' Mrs Tippett tried to calm them down.

Lauren and Chris looked interested and asked if it would be about the squirrel again. Mrs Tippett said no, but it was a tale from long ago and not very nice. This made them even more inquisitive so she knew she had their attention and I felt myself relax, knowing they would be quiet for a bit at last!

Mrs Tippett began by introducing the character of 'Old Smeller.'

'This story is about what happens to people who have given up and 'Old Smeller' was a very well-known local gentleman who lived in an old house in one of the still unmade roads that lead into Hockley Woods.

He had lived there for so long that no-one could even remember when he had moved in and not many people had occasion to go past his cottage because it was not on a main road and was a dead end that was full of pot-holes and overgrown with brambles and nettles. The milkman didn't come down there and nor did the postman because he never had a letter from anyone.'

'Didn't he get bills?' Lauren asked.

'Well, I suppose he did but I do know he only ever used candles and had an old wood-burning stove to cook on and keep warm by. He even had a well in the garden like so many people do around here. There are so many gardens with springs – where water comes up out of the ground - around Hockley and Rayleigh. I think he must have had to pay for something, sometimes though.'

'Oh yes, we've got a well and so have some of our friends,' Lauren said. 'There's also a bit of our garden where water comes out onto the lawn when it's been raining a lot too.'

'Yes, that's right,' Mrs Tippett continued. 'However, getting back to our story, you can tell he lived a very lonely existence.

Anyway, we often saw this man walking for miles around the district and over the years his appearance deteriorated and his clothing began to look very drab indeed. His beard got longer and longer and his hair got thinner and thinner. I swear he never washed anything. I think everyone felt sorry for him but actually no one seemed to care enough to visit him and check if he was all right.

Now, as you know, I lived in the middle of the woods in those days and I saw more than most people did who lived in the big houses on the main roads. I knew that this man was once a married man and when he moved here with his wife, they built their own house in what is known as the 'Colonial Style' with rooms around a central courtyard and a verandah (which is like a balcony) all round the outside. It was a very pretty house and I quite envied them. I think he may have been out in India or Malaya as a young man because he had lots of Oriental ornaments and beautiful carved chests.

You may wonder how I know all this and I will tell you a secret – I used to look through the windows when I knew they were out. I didn't do any harm, I was just curious.

One evening I happened to be walking past his home when I heard him crying and I stopped outside his gate wondering whether to go in or not but I thought it would be very rude. I never saw his wife again and I have no idea what happened to her. I think he must have had a broken heart and that's why he let himself go.

Well, the years passed and he got more and more eccentric and his garden became overgrown and his house fell into disrepair. Rumours started to go around about him saying he always did a wee in his trousers and that was why they were tied up with string at the bottom of each trouser leg. That wasn't true – they were tied up because he had an old bike that he used to ride into the village to get food. But still, people will say very cruel things and because he didn't wash very much he certainly did suffer with B.O. (That stands for body odour if you don't know – he never used a deodorant!). The cruel name of 'Old Smeller' became his nickname and children would actually shout that out when he walked past.

Now Lauren – I can see you smiling and yes, I suppose his name is quite funny but behind every man, woman and child there is a life and sometimes it is a sad life so you should think before you judge.

'Old Smeller' died a few years ago, I think he must have been nearly 100 years old and now his house has been rebuilt and all memory of him is fading fast. However, you can find his tombstone in the local church graveyard and there, you will find his real name with his nickname underneath so maybe people did remember him fondly after all.'

'What was his real name?' Chris asked.

'Ah now, I think I remember rightly that it was Albert Fortescue and I know that is quite a posh name which is probably why he was out in Malaya back in the twenties. A lot of young men went there to earn good money in the rubber plantations.' Mrs Tippett answered.

'What's a rubber plantation?' Chris asked.

'Why, it's where they get rubber out of rubber trees,' Mrs Tippett replied. 'Did you know that?'

'No.' Chris replied.

'Well, I am sure your mum will tell you all about it later because now I am tired and I think it must be time for you to have your tea. I hope you will remember this story and know that it is important to keep clean and tidy.'

I laughed at this and said I thought it would be a miracle if they did but what a brilliant tale it was and I was sure Lauren and Chris would never forget it.

Merlin

In the last few stories you have heard the name of our dog, Merlin, who was a very special type of Border collie. He had unusual colouring of grey and white with a bit of brown and had one blue eye and one brown eye. Some people are not sure if they like this or not because of the strangeness of having two different colour eyes. However, this can happen in people too and there are some famous people with eyes that are different.

Merlin was already part of our family and belonged to the children's uncle in Somerset. However, Uncle David had to move back into London away from the countryside and knew Merlin would pine for the open spaces. We offered Merlin a home and he arrived at our house a few days before Christmas. It must have been very bewildering for him especially as we already had Pebble. He was incredibly shy and used to hide underneath tables and behind chairs so all you could ever see was his shiny black nose!

After a while, he began to settle in but he was definitely a bit mischievous because he managed to get hold of our turkey which was slowly defrosting in the bath upstairs one morning and on another day he got all the sausages out of my shopping bag! I think he was being a bit rebellious like any teenager (in dog years he was about a year and a half old which is about 15 in human years).

As you know, he loved long walks in the woods but even more, he loved going to the big local country park where he was famous for his habit of literally bouncing up and down in deep grass. He would run for a bit then leap into the air and come down a bit further on and it made everyone laugh. I think he did it so he could see where he was going because he didn't do it anywhere else. He never went very far from my side though, I am sure he was worried about getting lost because he had moved so very far away from his original home. He was loved by all the family and got on really well with Pebble the Pointer and Humbug our very large, ginger tom cat. However, Pebble was much older than Merlin and sadly she went to Doggy Heaven at the grand age of 12 (which is quite old for a dog).

Merlin obviously missed Pebble's company so a new puppy was introduced to the family home and she was the softest, soppiest dog you can possibly imagine. Maisie was so girly and affectionate. She loved cuddly toys (which annoyed the children who had to keep rescuing soggy stuffed animals from her bed) and simpered over everyone who came to the house. She was an absolutely useless guard dog unless you count licking someone to death! However, she was fast as only a true Border collie can be and she was like lightning when she took off into the woods.

Maisie also led Merlin astray when we went on holiday to the Lake District one year by launching herself into complete sheep dog mode before we could catch her on a mountaintop. Before we knew it, she was about half a mile away and sending lots of sheep down towards a small, glacial lake. There was a lot of muttering from other walkers and we were told off for being irresponsible. Worse still, Merlin (who had always been such a well-behaved dog) thought this looked like great fun and ran after her and barked his way across to the other side of the valley. It took a lot of loud whistling and very stern shouting to bring them back to heel and it was collar and lead from then on!

In the year of Britain's last total solar eclipse which took place on 11th August 1999, we went on holiday to Devon in the Easter holidays. It was very cold and snowy that year and every outing saw us wrapped up in heavy coats, scarves and hats. One day we were larking about in the River Dart doing something I would definitely not recommend: jumping across all the big rocks and stones and you can probably guess what happened. Yes, I fell in and pulled Chris in with me! I know this was a bit silly and I can hear you all tut-tutting as you read this and shaking your heads. You will find out later that I was not a very responsible dog owner either but more in the paragraph after next.

Chris and I were very wet and had to sit in our car without our outer clothes on so we could dry out quickly with the car heater on maximum. It was snowing outside and the windows kept getting steamed up as we slowly defrosted in the back. Poor Dad could hardly see to drive and Lauren kept complaining that she was too hot

The next day was dark and grey and we took the dogs for a walk near to where we were staying. Suddenly, Maisie spotted a deer in the forest and ran after it. Merlin always followed her (as you know from the sheep-herding episode) wherever she went so he dashed in too. There was lots of barking as they ran further and further away but eventually Maisie re-emerged looking very wet and bedraggled. However, there was no sign of Merlin so we called and whistled and called again with no luck. He must have gone so far, he'd got lost. We tried not to panic and hoped he would find his way back to the garden when he ran out of steam.

The hours dragged by with no sign of Merlin. Maisie kept looking out of the window hopefully. By nightfall I was beside myself with worry and very tearful. The children couldn't sleep and it was a long, long night. The next day, there was still no sign of Merlin so we rang the local police, the Dartmoor Ranger service and the local newspapers to ask them to look out for him. They were all really kind but didn't hold out much hope

We had to return home to Essex without Merlin. It was the hardest thing we have ever done and everyone was silent on the journey. I think my heart was breaking and all we could do was gaze out of the car window in the vain hope that we might spot him.

For the next few weeks we tried everything possible to make the public aware of his being lost and we called random people in the telephone books throughout the north Devon area. We did eventually have a couple of sightings from people who said they had seen a dog answering Merlin's description and we plotted their locations on a map and realised he was travelling from north Devon across Dartmoor to south Devon. As these sightings came in we kept our spirits up that someone would be able to rescue him and we also continued making telephone calls to complete strangers in towns and villages in the south Devon area that could be on his route.

We heard that he came across a campsite on Dartmoor where some scouts gave him food and we also found out that he had visited a monastery on several occasions and they kindly gave him scraps but could not catch him.

They were the hardest three weeks you can possibly imagine and we spent day and night racking our brains about what to do and wondering if we should go and drive around Devon until we found him but that would have been madness because it is such a huge area.

But now I have to hand over to this remarkable dog to tell his story in his own words.

* * * * * * * * * * *

Hello. My name is Merlin. I come from a long line of blue-merle Border Collies in Somerset but now I live in Essex with a lovely family who really love me and make a fuss of me.

One of the great things about my family is that they take me on holidays and I see lots of new things and meet lots of new people. One of these holidays turned out to be a real adventure for me and I had some amazing experiences. Sometimes I was in danger and sometimes I was very lonely but it was very exciting.

It all started when I went off chasing deer with my best friend, Maisie. She gave up the chase really quickly but I kept running because I could just see them disappearing into the darkest forest I have ever been in. Suddenly, I realised I was completely on my own and all I could see was trees, trees and more trees. It was pitch black and eerily quiet. I tried not to panic and sniffed around to follow my tracks back to where I had started and where I knew my family was waiting. However, it had been snowing quite a bit and then thawing and the wet snow was making it hard to smell anything at all. I sniffed everywhere around in a big circle but was really uncertain which way to go. In the end I decided to keep going in a straight line until I came out of the forest and that way I knew I would find open spaces or even better, a house. If I could find someone kind, they might see my name tag and telephone my family.

It was getting very dark and when I emerged from the forest. I realised that I had ended up in farmland and there were only fields for mile upon mile and not a house in sight. I stood there for a while trying to decide what to do and not knowing which direction to travel. By the time night fell, I had nowhere to shelter so I just curled myself into a tight ball by a stone wall and rested as much as I could. All I dreamed about that night was warm fires, a big bowl of food and being stroked and fussed by the children. I was dreadfully unhappy.

The next day was freezing and snowing again but I kept walking, hoping to find some houses. At last I found a farm building but there were cows in the yard and they really frighten me with their huge faces and loud moos so I kept on until I found another farm where there were some people working outside. I was really excited and ran up to them barking.

'Get away, get away,' a man shouted.

'Go on with yer, you dirty hound. Keep away from our chickens,' another man yelled.

They threw stones at me so I scarpered fast.

'Oh dear, what on earth am I going to do?' I thought. 'Maybe they will all chase me away around here?'

I whimpered a bit and thought of Maisie and my family and whether they would be worrying about me. I listened hard to see if I could hear Mum's familiar whistle and I barked a bit just in case but all I heard were the distant barks of another dog I didn't recognise.

I kept walking towards the sun, which was just visible behind some low, grey cloud. I knew my family lived near the sea because we often went for walks there in the wintertime so I knew I needed to keep going south not north. If I kept going in that direction maybe I would find home or I could follow the coastline until I did. With this plan sorted out in my head I decided to put my best paw forward and start walking without bothering any more humans.

The first few days were really cold and full of sharp, biting winds but I always managed to find somewhere warm to snuggle up at night but soon the terrain became more and more desolate and uninhabited. On the third day I stumbled upon a river and it smelled familiar! As I followed it for a mile or two I suddenly found an area I recognised. I sniffed about and knew that the family car had been there and at the water's edge I found traces of both me and Maisie so I was really excited for a moment until I remembered that we were there days ago and not recently. Still, it was a comforting moment and made me more determined to keep going.

By now I felt like I was in the middle of nowhere because there were no farms, houses or towns and just a few sheep here and there who obviously ran away whenever I approached. I began to lose track of the days but I think it must have been about ten days after I got lost that I started to see more in the way of houses and people and late one evening I smelt some delicious bacon being fried which was like a magnet as I hadn't eaten in all that time. I saw some children and their tents and they were all laughing and shouting and obviously having a great time. I wondered if they would hear my tummy rumbling as I crept up as far as I dared to see if there were any bits of food lying around.

Then I heard a boy shout out, 'Hey, look at that poor dog over there, he looks lost!'

A few of the other boys turned round and looked at me and I tensed up ready to run away.

'Here boy, here boy, come and get some food.'

'Come on, don't be frightened. Would you like a bit of bacon?'

'Oh the poor thing, it's so thin.'

One by one they crouched down and called me to them so I felt a bit braver and hunkered down a bit so they would know I wasn't going to bite them. You never know, I probably looked like a wild animal! I almost grovelled at their feet when I arrived in the middle of their camp and tried very hard not to snap at the first hand that held out some food for me. It disappeared down my throat faster than you can say 'bacon and egg' so they soon found more food for me. By now, quite a few more had joined the crowd around me and I was a bit worried I might be in trouble but then an adult came over and he was really kind too.

'Well now boys, what have we got here?' He got down on his knees and gave me a gentle pat. 'So where did you come from chap? Have you come down off the moor?'

I obviously couldn't answer him but instead, I nuzzled into his hand and looked at him with my most appealing gaze.

'Hmm, you've got a collar and oh, here's your name and a number. Let's take a look.'

However, just as he started to look at my name on my collar an enormous noise startled me and I was so alarmed I literally dashed away as fast as I could. I ran and ran and then stopped to look back to see what on earth it was. There, coming down over the hills and swooping up again were two aeroplanes. I knew what these were because they flew over my home every day but back home they were really quiet compared to these monsters. They came down so low and went so fast and the noise was deafening. I was truly terrified. I heard them roaring off into the distance but then to my horror, they started to come back. I took off at breakneck speed, away from the roar until I came across more houses and roads and I stopped for a drink in the river.

There was a part of me that really regretted running away from the kind children and I knew that they would have seen my identification tag but there was no way I could go back now; I just had to keep on going.

I walked on for a few more days but managed to find food here and there in bins and outside restaurants late at night and eventually found myself in a beautiful valley where there were just a few sheep and hens by a small farmhouse. I saw a barn where I could sleep but just as I sneaked in the back door, I heard a lot of barking and for a moment I thought it might be Maisie. However, I turned round to see the prettiest Collie lady dog I have ever seen. I literally stopped dead in my tracks but then had a horrible thought, 'What must I look like?'

I think she could see my embarrassment and I swear she smiled as she turned away and walked down towards the river. Next thing I knew, she was walking out into the water and looking back at me as if to say, 'You need a wash!'

I followed her down and although I don't really like water, I stepped gingerly into the cold shallows and bravely dropped in up to my neck. The naughty girl then came bounding over to me and put her paws on my back and pushed me right in! Well, if that was her game, then I was not going to be such a push-over so I shook myself off as vigorously as I could to splash water into her eyes and then ran into her and pushed her back in! This went on for quite a while but then I heard some whistling and a voice calling out.

'Hey! Brimble! Come here. What's going on?' It was a lady calling out but I could tell she had a kind voice. However, I was a bit worried that she might tell me off so I ran off across the fields and decided to stay in the neighbourhood in case I could see Brimble again.

The next day I could hear Brimble barking and fussing around the sheep and I watched her from a distance as she cleverly rounded them up and herded them into some sheep-pens. All the sheep were being soaked in some very smelly medicinal water and complaining really loudly. It was quite comical to watch. Brimble was really busy but I think she could tell that I was around because I saw her stop and sniff the air a few times. I dozed in the early spring sunshine and late in the afternoon the lovely Collie woke me up with a delightful nudge and a big lick. I looked up into her eyes and I was in love.

I spent the next few days hanging around the farm waiting for any opportunity to meet up with Brimble who worked harder than any dog I have ever known. She made me feel very lazy but when we were together I forgot all my troubles. I told her what I was trying to do and she encouraged me by saying the sea was not that far away but she was very sad to know that I would have to leave her. We were both so much in love that when I knew I had to go I think it broke both our hearts. However, the days were slipping by fast and I had to keep on with my quest to find my family. I left her on a beautiful late April morning and kept looking back until she was just a black and white speck on the horizon.

As I walked over the next hill I was sure I could smell the sea. There was a warm wind blowing and it was quite misty but I started to see the odd seagull here and there. My pace quickened and I tried not to think about Brimble too much. Then, to my horror, I saw the first real obstacle in my path. Stretching out in front of me, as far as the eye could see, was an enormous road with thousands of cars roaring up and down it. It was the biggest road I had ever seen up close but I knew I had seen something like it from inside a car. There had to be a way to get across to the other side. I walked for miles in one direction and finally found another road that went underneath the scary road above. It was just a small lane and I felt much safer. A few miles further on, I came across another obstacle. Even more cars and buildings and people! It was like a whole town so I knew I would find plenty to eat. I was very nervous and the people were very unfriendly. Most of them had children so they shouted at me to go away so I obliged them quite happily.

I didn't like this place very much so I tried to find another route. Eventually I came across a lovely quiet park where very strange men were walking about in long dresses. They seemed very gentle and did make an effort to be friendly and leave food out for me but I was still miles from home and rescue and worn out with worry.

I felt so disorientated and had no idea how to get to the sea with so many big places in between. I walked between the shopping centre and the place with the men in dresses for a few days until I finally found my river again and I was really excited to get back on the path to the sea at last.

Finally, I arrived. It was so overcrowded with houses everywhere and people and cars and trucks and more people. I avoided them as much as possible and decided to go uphill as far as I could so I could see further and maybe even see home. I found myself high up on a cliff overlooking the sea with nothing else around for miles and miles. I literally dropped down with exhaustion and slept for hours.

The days went by in this strange high place. On three sides it was high cliff that made me feel quite ill looking down at the swirling sea below. Behind me, the way I had come, was a big car park with a café at the end so there were plenty of pickings to be had. I avoided people at this place because they nearly always had children and adults always shout at you as if they think you are going to eat them! As if I would! I love children, especially my own family.

The days were definitely getting warmer and I thought I really should be doing something about trying to find my way home but the pads of my feet were incredibly sore and kept bleeding every time I tried to walk on them. I knew I had to rest. I was also aware that my days in the fields meant I had some visitors in my fur and these nasty creatures were biting me all the time. I must admit I had lost all hope and I felt so weak and alone. I kept thinking about what my family would think if they knew I had given up on them.

One particularly busy day when there were far more people visiting the area than before, I crept out of my usual hiding place in the hedges because a poor baby boy had dropped an ice-cream cone and it was too good to miss. As I ducked back into my hidey-hole I heard a woman say, 'Hey, that's the dog that's been in all the newspapers! Quick. See if we can catch him.'

I wasn't sure what to do. I didn't know if she would help me and when she said, 'Catch me,' I thought she might lock me up somewhere and my family would never find me.

I crouched down low and growled a bit and that seemed to do the trick. I could hear her talking excitedly to her husband and saying things like, 'Call the police!' and 'We must try and get hold of him.' This made me even more nervous. I slunk away into the gorse bushes and hoped she wouldn't chase me. I sighed with relief when I saw her walk away and whined a bit too because I was more unhappy than ever.

That night was warm and gentle and all the stars were shining so I came out of my hiding place to enjoy the fresh air. The area was totally deserted and I sniffed around for any leftovers in the café. Suddenly I thought I heard someone whistling; it sounded so familiar I couldn't believe my ears. The whistling was very far away and came and went a bit but then I heard a car engine! It must have been about two in the morning and nobody ever came at that time of the night so my heart started to pound with anticipation. Then I saw a car just like the one belonging to my *family but I had to be careful so I hid away and watched warily. I saw a man get out and I was sure it was Dad but he was a long way off. I waited a bit, getting more and more excited because then a woman got out and started whistling and walking towards the cliff-edge. Oh I cannot tell you how overcome I was with emotion - I knew it was Mum but I just couldn't move my legs! I literally dragged myself out into the car park and fell at her feet in utter relief and tears were pouring down my face.*

Mum was feeling me all over saying, 'Is it really you Merlin, is it really you?' How could she not know? She shone a torch over me and looked puzzled. 'Merlin?' she asked again. I was stunned that she wasn't sure and thought she might have forgotten me because it had been so long. Then she shouted to Dad to come over quick and he ran to where we were sitting on the ground and said, 'Goodness me, it really is Merlin, I don't believe it, I don't believe it.'

They both hugged me and Dad picked me up as if I was just a feather and put me in the car. They were laughing and crying and fussing me and exclaiming about how thin I was. Then they mentioned the word that I dreaded more than any other – bath! However, even that couldn't spoil the moment and as they drove me home I slept and slept and slept knowing I was safe for the first time in over three weeks.

* * * * * * * * * * * *

It was a Bank Holiday Monday when we received a call from a lady who had seen Merlin on her walk on Berry Head in South Devon. She said he appeared to be very frightened so she didn't try to catch him in case he ran off. We knew we had to drive down that night and set off at about ten o' clock leaving the children with their older sister, Lisa. We arrived in the early hours not knowing what a huge area Berry Head Country Park was. We drove to the car park at the very end of the promontory and decided to wait until dawn before searching for Merlin. You cannot possibly imagine what it was like to drive 270 miles and have no idea that just one whistle would bring him right to your feet! It seemed like a miracle at the time.

Merlin was so footsore and covered in nasty sheep tics, which attach themselves to animals and make them very ill. In all, the vet found over thirty of these nasty things. We called the Western Morning Newspaper in Devon who had helped us by running his story and they could not believe he had been found in such amazing circumstances. Next thing we knew, we were inundated with telephone calls from newspapers, radio and TV stations and a freelance photographer dashed to our house to take Merlin's picture which appeared all over the country. He was famous! He appeared on the television and earned the headline of the day, 'Lost and Hound' in the Daily Express. We travelled up to London to appear on TV several times and Anglian TV kindly came to the house the day after we found him to film him in the garden.

He was terribly thin and it took a month or so to get him back to normal and to let him off his lead because we were so worried he might run off again. However, he soon returned to his old self and although he was always a bit quieter after his escapade, he was also very close to us and never let us out of his sight again.

After a few months though, he took to going off on expeditions and we always worried a bit. We found out from lots of people that he always took the same route across the woods. He went to the local school and liked watching the children and from there he went past the vet's surgery and library into town to have a look around the bins behind the local supermarket. Our vet would often see him sitting on the grass opposite his surgery eating a French stick or something out of a carrier bag! He became a local celebrity and much loved by everyone.

A little while after Merlin's homecoming, we received a letter from the owner of Brimble. He sent congratulations to Merlin on becoming a father! He wrote about how Merlin had been spotted around his farm late in April. Merlin and Brimble were the proud parents of six lovely puppies and they were all famous because everyone in the area knew about his epic journey.

We also heard from one of the monks in Buckfast Abbey who had tried to encourage Merlin to stay with them by feeding him lots of scraps. He told us that Merlin was too nervous to approach and although he loved the food, he always ran away.

Later that year, we returned to Devon to witness the spectacular total solar eclipse from a beach on the south coast. We then drove up to Berry Head to show the children where we found Merlin. The last time we were there it had been pitch black but in the daylight we realised just how huge the area was and also how high the cliffs were. We held on tight to Merlin and Maisie and wondered again at how incredible his journey was.

Merlin was definitely a magical dog that will never be forgotten. He has now joined Pebble in heaven and I am sure they are enjoying running and jumping in perfect green grass and lying in the sun on long lazy days. We still miss him.

The Superstitious Magpie

When spring is in full flow and the hawthorn trees start to blossom, the woods become a veritable hive of industry. Little animals are being born and the parents rush to and fro to gather food for hungry mouths. Everywhere there are signs of new life and the leaves are bright green and the sky is bluer than at any other time of year.

We were driving back from the shops one afternoon when a magpie flew in front of us and I instinctively saluted the bird to ward off bad luck. Faye asked why I did that every time I saw a magpie and I felt a bit foolish because I knew it was a superstition I had picked up from my mother. I tried to explain.

'Well I must admit it's a habit I picked up from my mum and I have been doing it all my life but every time I do, I feel a bit silly and try to stop myself. It's all to do with the rhyme, 'one for sorrow, two for joy' that you probably know and if you see one magpie on its own you are supposed to salute it. Apparently it is like a form of respect and you hope it won't bring you any sadness. Anyway, it's a stupid superstition and it doesn't mean anything at all so take no notice.'

'I like magpies,' replied Faye, 'I don't know why people say they don't.'

'I like magpies too,' Lauren piped up from the back seat. But that man on TV always shouts at them doesn't he?'

She was referring to her favourite programme on the television at the time which was an adaptation of a very famous book by Gerald Durrell called 'My Family and Other Animals.'

'Yes, the man does shout at them a lot but that's because they keep coming into the house and taking things. They can be very cheeky and they also have a reputation for taking shiny things so people call them "thieving magpies." They definitely get a bad press that's for sure.' I answered. 'Mind you I do know that in some countries they are considered to be good luck.'

'Do you think Mrs Tippett salutes magpies?' Lauren asked.

'I bet she knows tons about them,' Faye observed.

'Well we should go and visit her again so maybe we can ask her next time,' I offered.

'Ooo I like Mrs Tippett, she gives us cakes,' Chris finally joined the conversation. He was always hungry!

'OK, I'll give her a call when we get back,' I said.

A few weeks passed by and the Spring half term finally came so the children were all dying to go round to Mrs Tippett's house. Faye came with us as she had a day off work and wanted to meet the lady we had all been talking about and she was also interested to know what she thought about magpies. Faye had a real affinity with birds and they often took food from her hand. No one else in the family had this ability to be that close to animals but they were uncannily drawn to her. Faye often brought back various creatures home to nurture and nurse back to health if she found them in distress anywhere. She even kept a baby grass snake in her room over the winter months to stop it freezing to death!

It had been a while since our last visit and there was much to catch up on and a lot of excited chatter with all the children vying for attention. Finally, Faye found the opportunity to ask her questions.

'Mrs Tippett, do you like magpies?'

'Well there's a question! Of course I like magpies – they are a noble bird and very beautiful.'

'Why do so many people hate them then?' Faye asked. 'Everyone I know says they kill baby birds and bring bad luck.'

'Good grief! What an accusation. They may be people who live in towns and don't know about the laws of nature or maybe they are just repeating what they have been told which is not unusual. I often find that people are fond of making derogatory statements without ever bothering to check their facts.'

You could tell that Mrs Tippett was upset and angry with this subject and I did hope we hadn't stirred up a lot of bad feelings.

'I like magpies,' Faye replied proudly, 'and I think it's nasty to say all those bad things about them.

'Yes, you're right but do you know the rhyme about magpies?' Mrs Tippett leaned forward in her chair as she warmed to her subject.

'Yes,' Lauren and Faye answered together and then chorused:

One for Sorrow

Two for Joy

Three for a girl

Four for a boy

Five for silver

Six for gold

Seven for a secret, never to be told

'Why doesn't it go up to ten?' Chris asked.

'I think it does in some parts of the country because there are a lot of versions of this rhyme. However, where you may only see one magpie, if you wait, you often see another close by because a pair of magpies will stay together for life and one will pine for the other if it dies. The only time you may see them out on their own is in the spring when they are feeding their chicks or taking turns to sit on their eggs.'

'Mum always salutes magpies if they are on their own,' Chris shouted. I wished he hadn't said that because I felt a bit embarrassed.

'Don't worry dear, so many people are superstitious about them but have you ever thought they might be upset about the way we feel?' asked Mrs Tippett.

'Goodness no, I cannot imagine they even know do they?' I replied.

'Yes, they do and I will tell you why,' she answered mysteriously.

'Are you going to tell us a story?' Lauren asked excitedly.

'Yes, but it's not a story – all the things I tell you are true, you know that don't you?'

Faye looked suspicious so I gave a look as if to say, 'Don't say a word.'

Lauren and Chris nodded wisely knowing that everything Mrs Tippett told them was true and fascinating.

'Well then, this is what I heard when I lived in the woods many, many years ago.'

* * * * * * * * * * * *

On a lovely summer day, a visitor arrived in Hockley Woods who quite literally dropped out of the sky. A black and white flapping thing collapsed in a heap on the forest floor and at first glance appeared to be quite dead. On closer inspection, you could see little twitches and its feet made little running movements every now and then. The inhabitants of the trees looked down in puzzlement and wondered what it was. It definitely looked different but also familiar at the same time. There was the tell-tale black and white plumage and lovely blue-black tail but it was scrawny and bedraggled and very small compared to its cousins up above in the branches.

Word went round with loud 'caws' and 'croaks' and shouts of, 'Stranger in the woods!'

Bit by bit, more and more birds flew into the area and a few hopped down to inspect the poor thing more closely. He still didn't open his eyes or make any sound so they waited a while to see whether he would recover. A couple of smaller birds dared to draw closer because it wasn't often they could be in such close proximity to a magpie. Also, because he was so small and pathetic, they were not really in any danger.

'Do you think he's going to live?' asked a little wren (the tiniest bird in the woods).

'Well, he is still breathing,' replied a blue tit looking very cheerful (as they always do).

'I don't think he looks too good,' remarked a plodding wood pigeon who always tended to be pessimistic.

'Give him a prod and see if he wakes up,' suggested a cheeky sparrow.

The little birds were not at all sure about such a dangerous move so a bold robin flew down and landed on the stranger's back. He pecked at the poor Magpie's tummy and shouted, 'Wake up, wake up,' in his loudest voice.

There was a small sign of life and his mouth opened and closed a couple of times.

'He's trying to say something,' shouted a few baby blackbirds in their singsong voices. 'Listen. Quiet everyone, give him a chance,' they all called at once.

The strange magpie opened his beak and whispered, 'Lo.....,'

'What's that? What did he say?' A deaf old owl called down.

The little blackbirds called back, 'He said low.'

'Low what does he mean low? He couldn't get any lower, he's on the ground!' replied the owl sagely.

The pitiful bird tried to lift his head and whispered, 'Non. L'eau.'

'Well I don't know if he's right in the head,' the owl remarked. 'Now he's saying he's not low – what on earth is the matter with him?'

At this the grounded magpie struggled up onto his feet and said in a stronger voice, 'L'eau, je desire l'eau. Stupide oiseau.'

At this all the birds exclaimed at once.

'He's squawking mad he is.'

'What's that funny accent?'

'He's talking gibberish.'

'Did he just say stupid?'

'I don't think he's from around these parts – maybe he comes from up north?'

A tiny little voice piped up from high up in the treetops, 'Don't be silly you lot, he's from France. I know because I've been there and they all talk like that. My dad knows a bit of French so I'll go and get him.'

'Oh it's that snooty family of chiffchaffs that spend every winter in the south of France. They think they're so above us. Trust them to know,' a grumpy crow said with a shrug of his wings.

'Well at least they are being helpful,' replied a fellow crow who was nowhere near as bad mannered.

Eventually, the young chiffchaff (whose name was Cyril) came back with the rest of his family who were really curious to see who the visitor was. 'There he is Dad,' said Cyril pointing at the bedraggled pile of feathers on the forest floor. 'He looks very poorly.'

'Oh yes son, he does. Let's get a closer look.' Charles Chalfont Chiffchaff walked over and spoke very charmingly to the magpie. 'I say old fellow, are you from France? Pardon me, êtes vous Français?' he enquired.

'Ooo hark at him, all toffee nosed and speaking the lingo,' called out the grumpy crow from above.

'Shut up Harry,' everyone called back.

The little magpie looked pathetically up at Charles and replied, 'Oui, je suis Français.'

'Wee – he wants a wee!' laughed the baby blue tits and sparrows all together.

'Hush children,' cautioned the blue tits' mother. 'You can see he's in a bad way and he must be very frightened by us all staring at him.'

They looked guiltily down but still crowded round the visitor.

Meanwhile, Charles was coaxing the French magpie towards the stream that runs through the middle of the woods so he could get a drink. It was slow going but eventually he slid down the bank to the water's edge and sipped weakly for a while. All the other birds had followed him and there was quite a gathering by now.

Finally, with a bit of his strength restored, the visiting magpie climbed up the bank and stood in front of every bird encircling him.

'Bonjour, je m'appelle Maurice,' he said in a very strong accent.

Now, if you are wondering what on earth he said or even more how he pronounced it then you will be glad to know that every single bird there was also puzzled and standing open-beaked in astonishment.

'Eh, what was that? What did that peculiar bird say?' enquired Oscar the owl.

'He said something about apples I think,' the wren said helpfully in her tiny chirrup.

Charles looked a bit helpless as they all turned to him for a translation and the magpie looked hopefully at him thinking he could help.

'To be honest, that's got me stumped and he talks so fast I have no idea what he's on about,' he told them all. 'I'll ask him to speak more slowly.'

'Okay,' he said, 'Slow down a bit and tell us again. Lentement s'il vous plait.'

The bird looked quizzically at him and started again, 'Je m'appelle Maurice – I ..... am .... Maurice.'

'Hey he can speak English,' the other magpies cheered. 'Hello Maurice, glad to meet you!' cried one of them.

Maurice carried on, 'Je suis - pardonnez-moi - I am .... from France.'

'Yes we know that,' said Harry Crow sarcastically. 'What are you doing here then?'

Maurice looked up at him and made a funny noise that sounded a bit like he was blowing a raspberry but we know it couldn't possibly be! However, you could tell it was a bit rude!

'Who iz dis rude bird?' he asked. 'Tell 'im I try to speek.'

'Ooo don't fly off your handle!' Harry snorted back and then laughed, 'Ha ha, fly off your handle, ha ha, good one that.'

All the other birds tutted and muttered and made comments like, 'How rude,' and 'No breeding.'

But Harry was not put off in the slightest and continued with his wise-cracking by saying, ''Ere this bird is speaking pidgin English, ha ha ha ha ha.' And he laughed so much he fell backwards off his branch and looked extremely foolish. The others looked on shaking their heads in complete disappointment at his dreadful behaviour.

If you are not sure what pidgin English is or why this was a joke to all the birds you need to understand that it was meant as a pun (or play on words) and pidgin sounds the same as pigeon (the bird) and means a common basic language used between two different nationalities.

Charles asked him to tell everyone why he was here and how far had he flown and could he manage to speak in English?

'Yes, I can do,' Maurice began. 'But I vill 'ave to do it lentement – slowly - je m'excuse.'

He then settled down to start his story, which was so interesting, all the birds quietened down and even a hedgehog crept up to listen behind them. He couldn't really see the magpie very well but that didn't matter to him.

Maurice said he had flown for almost ten days to get to England and that is incredible for a magpie because they are not very good fliers. As you may know, they tend to glide from place to place rather than fly for any distance and there is a very good reason for this, as you will find out. They are incredibly shy and nervous birds and the reason for them darting from one safe place to another is born out of generations of magpie families avoiding hunters and it is this fear that explains why Maurice had fled to England.

Maurice and his wife and six children lived in southern France very near the Pyrénées which are the mountains between France and Spain. He told the gathering that the last winter was extremely bad and they almost starved to death. It was always very hard to survive in this part of the world because so many men tried to shoot magpies because they thought they brought bad luck. All the magpies around him agreed and looked at each other because they knew this was true in England too. Maurice told them that they were always very nervous when they saw men on their own out in the fields because that meant they were out hunting. One day his wife was trying to find food for her hungry babies when a horrible farmer shot and killed her as she tried to grab some of the chicken feed.

Everyone looked horrified at this and they were all very sympathetic.

Maurice carried on with his story. 'The farmer flung her out into the fields and I managed to pull her into the woods nearby. All my friends joined me with lots of beautiful leaves and grass to cover her over and soft moss to put under head so she could sleep in peace. I stood by her side for days on end crying my heart out and also protecting her from wild animals. In the end my friends told me I must pull myself together for the sake of my children and also because I had not eaten in all that time. It was a terrible tragedy and I was left on my own to bring up the children,' he said mournfully.

'Of course, I did my very best and they grew up fine and strong and I encouraged them to move nearer to a town where there would be more food and not so many guns. As for me, there was no reason to stay either so I decided to leave too. My beautiful wife was gone and I missed her so much.'

'You poor thing,' said one of the resident magpies. 'Me and my husband have been with each other for nearly ten years now and I would be lost without him.'

'Yes, marriage is for life and life's not much good without your partner is it?' another agreed.

'Yes, I agree,' said Maurice. 'Dat is why I wanted to move away so I could make a fresh start. I had heard from a travelling swallow that stopped by on his way from Africa who said that it was much nicer in England and that he could show me the way as far as the south coast if I wanted. I decided to join him but of course, I was much slower than 'im but he was very patient with me.

Ven I arrived in England I was very tired and hungry so I stayed a while in some high hills and started to learn your language. I think I am doing very well n'est ce pas?

'Owever, the people 'ere were also a bit strange and I found myself getting very anxious whenever I saw a human. They kept bringing their arm up to their head when they saw me and I always thought it was going to be because they were going to shoot me. I always say, "One for Sorrow," when I remember what 'appened to my wife. It 'as made me very superstitious I can tell you. I always dip down quickly when I see them do that thing. And they always shout at me when I try and help myself to the food they put out for us. They don't mind the other birds coming into their gardens but not magpies and I don't know why.

Then one day, I was looking for food in a back garden when I saw a lovely bright thing that I thought would look very nice in my home so I checked to see if anyone was around and then flew off with it. Next thing I knew, there was a lot of shouting from some humans and they were pointing at me and throwing things in my direction. I didn't understand what was wrong and I hid up high in my tree. The shiny object was so pretty and when I held it up it made lots of bright reflections in my nest. Then, to my 'orror, I heard a really loud noise and saw flashing blue lights coming up under my tree. I was scared stiff I can tell you.

Then dis man started floating up towards my nest on a big stick and lots of people were shouting and pointing in my direction.

'Quick, get up there!'

'I'm sure my diamond ring will be in its nest,' a girl shouted.

'These pesky magpies are such thieves,' a man swore.

Merde! I flew off as fast as I could I was so frightened and never looked back. It was truly terrifying. So dat is 'ow I come to be 'ere. I just kept flying until I found some place to hide and I saw all dese trees and knew it would be a good place to lie low.'

'That's an amazing story,' said Charles.

'Well you are very welcome here,' said Harry who was actually quite impressed by this brave magpie.

'I think he's very handsome and brave,' a lady magpie called Penny shyly said to her friend.

'Wings off!' she replied, 'I saw him first!'

'Well, I thought you were already spoken for,' Penny laughed.

The hedgehog strolled into the middle of the crowd and made an announcement. 'I think this is the bravest bird I have ever met and I sincerely hope you will tuck him under your wing and take care of him.'

They all laughed at his clever pun and agreed that of course they would.

'Well, I think you will probably be better off with your fellow magpie friends here than with me. For one thing, you like nests so high up it makes me feel a bit giddy and I like them a bit closer to the ground,' Charles suggested.

'Oui, dat would be very nice,' Maurice said and with that he winked at Penny and she giggled non-stop all the way back to her nest.

* * * * * * * * * * * *

Mrs Tippett finished her tale and looked at all of us with a twinkle in her eye.

'Is that really true?' Chris asked.

'Of course it is,' she replied. 'You don't think I made it up do you?'

Everyone laughed and said how much they had enjoyed the tale and Mrs Tippett told them to help themselves to more cakes.

'You do know that magpies have a bad reputation because of many ancient superstitions that are just not based on fact don't you?' She looked at us intently and we all nodded wondering what she was going to say.

'Well, all birds get hungry and all birds do eat other small animals and that is the way of nature and we are all part of the food chain. You will learn about that in school I am sure. Sometimes we think nature is cruel and barbaric but if you stop and think about it sensibly you will look at yourselves and see that we do the very same thing.

I expect you watch the wildlife programmes on the television so you will know that every creature in the world needs to survive and some may only eat grass but others will hunt other animals to eat. You must not get upset about it. We have an amazing, wonderful world to live in and everything is perfectly balanced and in harmony. You children have a duty to make sure that it always stays that way and to protect every living thing on earth so I hope you will remember that.'

We had never seen Mrs Tippett being so serious. We all agreed and felt a bit flat after her funny story. However, she didn't stay that way for long and suddenly laughed out loud and said, 'So next time your Mum salutes a magpie, tell her not to frighten it so much!'

Jack

Jack is probably one of the luckiest dogs you have ever met. It may be because of his rugged good looks and charm or it may be he does have the luck of the Irish but it is definitely true to say that he is very thankful that he is still alive.

It is very sad that there used to be so many stray dogs in Ireland who never found homes but every now and then some were brought to England to see if a family could be found to adopt them. These fortunate few were often taken to Battersea Dogs Home because they are visited by many thousands of families every year who want to help rescue an unwanted canine friend. We are one such family and we found and fell in love with our friend from over the water some years ago. He is so much a part of the family now and has a special place in our hearts.

When we visited Battersea Dogs Home in London we had no idea what we were looking for. We simply knew we wanted to look after a dog that desperately needed someone to take care of them. After wandering round and seeing so many poor furry creatures that looked at us appealingly, we still hadn't made up our minds and were just about to give up when a lady asked us if we had very young children. By now, Chris was eleven so we said no, we didn't. She smiled and asked if we were prepared to take on a dog that needed a bit of extra attention and we doubtfully said, yes, we were very used to dogs and thought we could help.

She then asked us to meet a dog that was very special indeed who actually lived in their office. We were introduced to a very shy and nervous collie-terrier cross who had lovely ginger and white colouring and silly big ears that didn't quite match his body size. The lady explained that he had been in rehabilitation and was quite difficult because he tended to nibble people's hands and that could frighten very young children. She explained it was a nervous habit that he was gradually overcoming but we would need to keep up his training.

We were all very excited and loved him straight away and we asked where he had come from. She explained that he had been running wild in a pack of dogs in Ireland and was lucky to be alive. That made us want him even more so we were interviewed at length and went back the following week to spend more time with him as a family and then to take him home when we all agreed he was the dog for us.

The night we took Jack home he paced up and down all evening and seemed very reluctant to settle down. We did wonder if he would be happy with us. However, after a few weeks, we knew he was going to be fine and we noticed how close he was to Chris. This may have been because poor Chris was having to use crutches at the time and was limping badly from a nasty rugby injury. I think Jack knew he was in pain as animals often do, so they formed a very strong bond immediately.

We were due to go on holiday later that year but not able to take Jack with us as it was such a long way by train and we worried about what to do until we had an idea.

'Why not ask Mrs Tippett if she knows someone who can look after him?' Chris suggested.

'You mean ask if *she* will look after him,' laughed Lauren.

'Oh I don't think so, she's getting on a bit and may find it too much,' I said.

'You could ask her,' Dad said. 'She must know someone who could.'

'OK then, I will. You never know.'

I called her and told her about our new member of the family and explained that we needed someone to help care for him for a few weeks.

'Oh how lovely, a new friend to get to know. How old is he?'

'They think he is just over a year old but fully-grown,' I replied.

'Ah, he's just a baby then,' she said. 'Would you mind if I offered to have him? I would take great care of him and we could have some lovely walks while I find out where he's come from and what his story is.'

I thought she was joking of course but you never did know with this intriguing old lady. Sometimes I swear I thought she could read your mind and animals' minds too for that matter!

'Ah, you're wondering if I am going batty aren't you?' she said, reading my mind.

'No, no of course not but I did wonder if it might be too much for you and that's why I was suggesting someone else if you knew anyone,' I hurriedly blurted out, not wanting her to know what I thought.

'Well, there's life in the old girl yet,' she giggled like someone a quarter her age and I wondered just how old she really was.

'Well if that's okay with you then we will be very happy for you to have him.'

It was all arranged and soon it was time for us to take Jack round to her house with his bed, lead and bits and pieces. Mrs Tippett looked overjoyed to see him and showed him into his new holiday home. She spoke to him like a child.

'Now Jack, this is going to be your home for a few weeks while your family goes on holiday and you and I are going to be great friends.'

She crouched down low and whispered something in Jack's ridiculously large ear, which pricked up while she spoke. Jack sat down and offered her his paw, which was one of his party pieces and they shook hands like humans. It was very comical. Naturally, Mrs Tippett responded by giving him a biscuit.

'Oh dear, please don't spoil him too much while we are away,' I warned, 'otherwise he will want the same treatment from us when we get back.'

Jack and Mrs Tippett both looked at me and then at each other as if to say, 'Oh doesn't she fuss!'

I gave him a hug and left quickly to hide the fact that I was a bit tearful at leaving him behind but no sooner had I turned to go out of the door than I heard lots of laughter and barking and shouts of 'Come on Jack! Let's go for a walk!' I knew he was going to have a great time.

Jack's Story:

My family went on holiday for a few weeks and I stayed over at Mrs Tippett's house. She is a very kind, old lady who listened to my story and was very sympathetic. She seemed to have an uncanny knack of knowing just what I was thinking and I hadn't realised until day three of my stay that she really did understand me. We were both dozing in the late afternoon sun one day and I was thinking about how far I had come and wondering what had happened to my companions back in Ireland when she suddenly said, 'Jack, you mustn't mourn for your old friends. They are all fine and happy and doing well.'

I jumped out of my fur in surprise. Surely she couldn't have had a clue what was on my mind? But then she carried on, 'Do you want to tell me all about it? Come and sit up with me on the swing seat and we'll have a lovely cuddle and you can tell me all about yourself.'

I looked at her with disbelief. Sit on the seat with her? I wasn't allowed to do that! But the word 'cuddle' tempted me so much because I did so love being petted. She patted the chair invitingly so I hesitantly jumped up and twirled round and round a bit until I got comfortable. It was very soft and cosy. I looked up at her waiting to see what she would say.

'Are you surprised that I can understand you?' she asked me.

I answered, 'Yes, but I have been able to communicate with some other people before but most of the time they are too fond of the sound of their own voice to really listen to me.'

'Yes, that's true. Human beings are always so busy aren't they?'

I nodded and smiled up at her. At least she had the time to take notice of me. I told her how my Dad always talks to me when we are on our own together and how I sit with him when he is busy making music in his studio. 'I really love music and I would love him to write a song about me one day.'

'You should tell him that,' she replied.

'I would love it to be a song with the Irish penny whistle in it because it reminds me of home.'

'Oh yes, I love Irish music too – especially the jigs which get your feet dancing.'

'I used to sit outside the bars in Ireland hoping for scraps of food and I knew there would be much more to eat after a party.'

'For how long were you straying?' she asked me gently.

'All my life until I was brought to England but it wasn't really straying – there was a whole crowd of us and we had some great times. Then again, we did have some miserable times too.'

'What happened to your parents?' Mrs Tippett enquired.

'I don't really know, I hardly remember my mum and I never met my father,' I said sadly.

'Can you remember where you were born?'

'Oh yes, it was as far west as you could possibly be on the Beara Peninsula with mountains and sea and soft, warm air. It was beautiful.'

'It sounds lovely, what a wonderful place to live. Do you miss it?'

'Yes, but I would much rather be here with all my lovely friends and a warm house to live in and food every day. I used to be chased away wherever I went before.'

Mrs Tippett asked me to tell her all about my old home and while I remembered it I felt like I was there because the memories were so vivid. It was incredibly green and quite uninhabited and the mountains were high and the lakes and sea were so blue.

* * * * * * * * * * * *

My mother disappeared one day when she went foraging for food in a local village. She didn't like going near people but she had hungry mouths to feed. When she didn't come back, we were all so hungry and frightened we decided to go and look for her. We were only about two months old and very inexperienced. I had two brothers and one sister but I hardly remember their faces now. When we were near the houses we huddled very close together thinking there would be safety in numbers but we were wrong. Before we knew it, a van pulled up sharply beside us and two people jumped out of it with big nets. I knew they were trying to catch us and we ran in all directions. I didn't stop to look back but I heard my brothers and sister yelping. Incredibly, I managed to escape.

As the van drove away I could hear them all crying out to me and I wondered if I had done the wrong thing. If we had all stayed together, then at least we would be able to help each other but then again, where were they going? I quickly ran off back into the countryside to think about what to do.

I managed to slip in and out of the village very easily over the next few weeks and always managed to find food and then one day, I was just having a nice nose around some bins when I heard a very gruff bark behind me and it went very dark. I nervously looked round and all I saw were four grey legs and paws. I looked up and up and up into the eyes of the tallest dog I had ever seen!

'Hello little pup, are you ok?' she kindly asked me.

'Ye-e-e-es I am, thank you,' I stammered back.

'Pleased to make your acquaintance. My name is Winifred.' She leant down towards me and gave me a gentle snuffle with her very large nose.

'M-m-m-me too. My name is Kenny.' I politely replied but cowered away a bit because she was just so enormous.

'I expect you are wondering why I'm so tall?' she laughed. 'Everyone does. I am a Wolfhound and I think you must be a bit of a cross.'

'I'm not cross,' I said indignantly.

'No, I don't mean that sort of cross silly, I said you are a cross. Do you know about your parentage? Was your father a terrier? You certainly have unusual colouring.'

'Oh, I don't know,' I replied, feeling foolish. 'I remember my mother, she was a Collie but I never met my Dad.' I actually felt a bit ashamed about this, as if I was less of a dog. What with calling me a 'cross' and asking me about my parents, I really felt inferior.

I think she realised this and she put a paw on my shoulder and her head on one side and said, 'Now, now little one, no need to get your tail in a twist. I didn't mean any harm and I'm really not in a position to have any airs and graces. My owners threw me out when I was only six months old. They said they couldn't afford to keep feeding me! I ask you. People! Hrmph! They take you in - they throw you out when they get bored. It's the same old story the world over.'

I felt a bit happier then and decided I liked her in a tall, gangly sort of way. She wasn't exactly a picture book herself with her coat all tangled and matted but she did have such kind eyes and her eyebrows kept going in all directions. It made her appear quite comical. She asked me if I would like to tag along with her and I said yes: I really wanted some company. As we strolled along she proved to be incredibly funny and knew lots of jokes.

She started off with, 'What do you get if you cross a dog with a vegetable? A Jack Brussel! Ha ha ha.'

I groaned inwardly as she started off with the next one:

'What do you get if you cross a sheepdog with a rose? A Collie-Flower of course! Isn't that brilliant?' She laughed at her own jokes, which made me laugh too and it made the world seem a much nicer place. That night we had a small feast of leftovers from the local inn and the last of the season's wild blackberries to finish. We lay down in the starlight and watched the full moon rise over the mountains and everything seemed perfect even though we were homeless.

'What's that really bright star?' I asked Winifred.

'That's Sirius, the Dog Star and it's in the constellation of Canis Major which means Big Dog,' Winifred answered knowledgeably. I don't know how she knew so much stuff and I wondered if she was just pulling one of my legs so I asked her how she knew.

'Oh my family used to watch so much television – it's amazing what you can learn and I loved documentaries. Have you seen a television Kenny?'

'No, what's that?'

'Gosh, you have led a sheltered life but then I keep forgetting you have never had an owner have you poor thing. Well it's a box shaped thing with pictures in it and people inside talk to all the people in the room. Well, you'll understand if you ever see one.'

I wondered about this and about having an owner and part of me thought it sounded nice but another part remembered how Winifred had been thrown out so I wasn't too sure about humans really. However, as the nights were getting colder I did think of being inside in front of a nice warm fire quite a lot.

Winifred and I decided to travel on a bit to try and find a larger town with more to eat and the next day we set off in an eastward direction. When nightfall came, we hadn't found any food and our bellies were rumbling. We found a small copse and sheltered together by a fallen tree for warmth. Suddenly, in the middle of the night, we heard barking and shouting and a lot of commotion. We huddled down low and peered out into the blackness.

'That was a close one Rory,' a deep voice boomed.

'Yeah, he was really angry wasn't he?' This was said in a very girly voice.

Another voice joined them, which was very high and squeaky, 'But we've got all the sausages, hee hee.' There followed a lot of wheezing and coughing. 'I am so out of breath from all that wunning.'

'Now then, now then fellas, we need to share our booty out fair and square,' the deep voice warned and it went very quiet. In fact it was so quiet we could sense them sniffing the air and we knew we would be discovered.

'Steady chaps,' said the deep voice. 'I think we've got company.'

Winifred whispered to me that we should be really brave and come out of hiding so we crept out together and stood there feeling very nervous.

'Oh ay. Who have we got here then? Looks like a Wolfhound and a mongrel lads. What shall we do with them?'

I do wish people would stop calling me names and I spoke up boldly, 'Sir, this is Winifred and my name is Kenny. We were only sleeping here for the night.'

'Oh yes and how do we know you weren't trying to ambush us for our food?'

'Sir, we didn't even know you would come here, it was deserted when we arrived.'

'Yes, good point, but you're a cheeky one aren't you?' he boomed.

'Yes, he's got spiwit he has,' said the wheezy dog who obviously had trouble with his R's.

'I like him,' said the girl-dog who looked quite cute, even in the dark.

'Well come over a bit closer so we can sniff you,' said the big dog.

Winifred and I timidly walked over and waited, while everyone in the wood inspected us.

'I think they'll do. Let me introduce myself. My name is Bryan.' We could now see to whom the deep voice belonged and it was very *hard not to laugh. Bryan was a small Beagle about thirty centimeters tall and full of his own importance, which puffed him up a bit.*

The other two dogs came over and took turns to say hello.

'My name is Wowy,' said Rory who turned out to be a large Dachshund.

'And my name is Cathleen and I am very pleased to meet you.' Cathleen was the most beautiful dog I had ever seen. 'I am an Irish Terrier and I detect we may be related little man.' She addressed this to me and I blushed terribly and was very thankful it was still quite dark.

'I think we'd better share our food out with our new friends. I know, I know, it means less for us, but we have to behave in a civilised manner,' Bryan said, giving us a sausage each.

We all sat quietly looking at each other while we enjoyed our small feast and knew we were going to be good friends.

From that night on, we travelled together from place to place and had such a laugh. I know that Cathleen was a bit old for me but she was definitely more like a girlfriend than a mother. Winifred took that responsibility for us and was always fussing and being very sensible. She taught us good manners and how to keep ourselves clean and was very fussy about our toilet habits. Every day she would ask us if we were going normally because she said that would be the first sign if we were ill. It was a bit embarrassing but she really did know a lot of stuff about medical things because she was the only dog that had ever visited a vet.

Winifred drove us all mad with her jokes of course and seemed to have one for every occasion, including meeting Rory.

'I say Rory! Why did the Dachshund bite the woman's ankle?' she asked him. 'Because he couldn't reach any higher ha ha ha ha!'

Rory did not look impressed. 'Are you mocking my stature madam? I am quite tall compared to my welations thank you.'

Little did he know that we were laughing at the way he spoke, not his height but no one dared give the game away!

Every day we managed to find something to eat and most days we were chased by angry butchers, grocers and shop-keepers but it was such fun and we never worried about being caught: apart from Rory because he couldn't run as fast as us. Our favourite places to find food were the local pubs or inns because everyone was friendlier and often threw us scraps. I loved sitting outside listening to the music and the bands that played most nights. However, our good luck was about to run out and Winifred told us that she overheard someone talking outside the newsagents saying there was a 'pack of dogs running wild and they must be caught.'

For a while we tried to stay out of sight and only came out at night to look for food but by now it was winter and cold and wet. We were so hungry and fed up with being outdoors in all weathers. However, every time we went into towns or villages we risked being caught and I was so terrified of this happening to me and always thought about what had happened to my family. I often wondered about what had become of them and I know I cried in my sleep because Cathleen would comfort me in the night with lovely snuggly cuddles and tell me that everything would be all right. Then one day I saw my first snow and we all realised our situation was dire.

'Maybe we should turn ourselves in?' suggested Winifred.

'And then what? We'll all be put down,' Bryan said gloomily.

He was right. We'd all heard the rumours and knew what fate awaited stray dogs like us. It was our worst fear.

'But we can't cawwy on like this, we're all going to die of starvation or cold anyway,' retorted Rory, ever the pessimistic canine.

'Maybe he has a point,' Winifred mused. 'It's only a matter of time till we are caught and winter has only just begun. Maybe we would be better off handing ourselves in?'

There was a lot of arguing that day and with no consensus of opinion by nightfall, we soldiered on as best we could until one day, one fateful day, the decision was taken out of hands.

We had wandered into the outskirts of a very large city where it was sheltered and had plenty of places for us to hide out. We had been there a few days when we started to meet other strays who warned us about the dog wardens who were patrolling everywhere picking up homeless creatures - not just dogs but cats too - and they were never heard of again. This news sent a chill down my spine. We skulked around in pairs rather than all together to avoid drawing attention to ourselves and I naturally went everywhere with Cathleen.

One of these forays led us into a part of the city we had never been to before where the buildings were bigger than any we had seen before. It was very clean and there was no food to be had but what we didn't know was this was the sort of place where our kind definitely did not belong. We had just decided to turn in a different direction when we heard the squeal of brakes behind us and we absolutely ran for it. We didn't need to look behind us - we knew we were being chased.

We ran into a cul-de-sac and knew we were trapped. We turned round and tried to look fierce which was quite hard for both of us. In fact, we were trembling like a couple of frightened rabbits. We growled our deepest growls as two men approached us with nets and tried desperately to see if we could slip past them. Somehow, I think we both knew this was it and the men were not quite as scary as we thought they would be as they tried to talk to us kindly and patiently.

'Come on then you two, don't be frightened, we're here to help,' one of the men said.

'You try for the little mongrel Dave and I shall go for the terrier,' the other said.

I whispered to Cathleen, 'I'm going to turn myself in. I'm so tired of running and being cold.'

I sensed her agreement even though her body language said she was as tense as can be.

We let the men come right up to us and they hunkered down onto their haunches to put out their hands to us to let us know we could trust them. Thank goodness they didn't need to use their horrible nets.

'Well I'll be blowed, Gary. These poor things are turning themselves in!'

'Incredible. They must be so weak with hunger.'

They scooped us up and put us in their van, which looked more like a cage and we felt very trapped when they shut the door. Cathleen whimpered and put her head down between her legs and all I could see were her beautiful, dark eyes looking up at me questioningly. I felt so responsible and suddenly very panicky. What if they were going to split us up? Suddenly, I really regretted giving in so easily.

I put a paw on her back and nuzzled her reassuringly but couldn't find any comforting words to say.

* * * * * * * * * *

At this point in my story I felt I couldn't go on and Mrs Tippett somehow sensed my emotional state and suggested going for a run. A run, that made me laugh, because the thought of this dear lady running was so amusing.

'Oh, so you think I'm past it, do you?' She poked me in my side, 'Well I'll show you, come on chap.'

We strolled down the road towards the park and woods near to where she lived and I was surprised to see that she had quite a spring in her step. As we neared the woods she suddenly said, 'Come on then Jack let's go for a proper run!'

I needed no persuasion to set off at a fair pace but soon found lots of new smells and places to explore and of course, every time I stopped, Mrs Tippett caught up! That was her clever ploy to keep *pace with me! We had a lovely long explore and it really cheered me up and made me remember how glad I was to be alive.*

We returned to the house and Mrs Tippett asked me to carry on if I felt ready. I had a long drink and a bit of her toast and we settled back down.

* * * * * * * * * * *

After the dog wardens put us in the van, we were taken to a large building and put in a big cage together which made us feel a bit better. We could hear the barking and whining of lots of other dogs all of whom were calling to each other to check that they were all okay. There was a lot of reassuring chatter between us all and lots of news too. Cathleen and I could hear things like:

'Don't worry mate, you are going to a great home.'

'Cheer up old man, they will find someone to look after you.'

It seemed to be a temporary place to stay where new homes could be found for strays and we hoped for the best.

The next day we saw a lot of people who stared at us in our cages and we did our best to look friendly and appealing but I am sure we looked pretty bedraggled and wild. However, late in the afternoon, a woman stopped by and stared at us for ages and then came back with two children. They were talking excitedly about Cathleen but didn't seem to be taking much notice of me. I feared the worst and the worst happened. The wardens came into our cage and put a lead on Cathleen and tried to pull her out. She began to panic and dug her feet in as hard as she could and started crying. I was crying too and I tried running at the men to make them let go. Before I knew it, they had taken her away and the last thing I heard was her calling back to me.

'Kenny, Kenny, I don't want to leave you!'

'Cathleen, oh Cathleen, please forgive me.'

'Of course I do, I love you. I will always love you Kenny.'

Those were the last words she said to me and it was the last time I saw her.

After a few days of sitting in my cage, crying and howling and finding no comfort, another man came round looking at all the dogs that were in the building and he wrote lots of notes on a big piece of paper. He looked kind and he spoke to me in a very quiet voice, 'Don't you worry, we'll take good care of you.'

I didn't know what he meant and hoped it would be good news. You heard so many rumours about dogs disappearing and never being seen again.

Days went by and suddenly, one bright summer morning, there was a lot of commotion and barking and before I knew it, the door was opened and a girl came in with a lead and led me outside to another van. Quite a few of us were put inside and I could hear everyone shouting out.

'What? Where are we going?'

'Oh please tell us it's not the end.'

'I'm frightened.'

'Don't wowwy fwiends. I think we are going on a fewwy to England.'

I yelled out, 'Rory, is that you!'

'Yes! It's Rowy here. Who's that? Is that Kenny?'

'Yes, it's me! How do you know we are going to England?'

'Yes, how, how, how,' howled all the other dogs in the van.

'Because I heard them talking the other day. It's a chawity that wescues dogs and takes them to new homes in England.'

'Wescues? Chawity? What is that dog saying?' someone called out.

'Don't you dare tease him, that's my friend and he's very clever,' I answered.

'Well, that sounds like an adventure. I hope we can find homes there,' a nice girl dog said.

There was a lot of chatter and excitement and then we saw the doors open and we could smell salty air. We were by the sea! Then a few men and women came and took us out one by one and led us up a steep bridge onto a ship. I had never been on a ship before, of course, but I knew what it was straight away. For a moment, I forgot my troubles and felt really excited. We were all taken below decks and given food and water and a soft bed each. I think we were all nervous and it was very strange being in a room that rocked and rolled around.

Suddenly there was an enormous noise of a horn being sounded and we could hear deep engine noises. Then the movement of the ship really increased and I felt a bit sick. Quite a few dogs actually were.

The journey seemed to last forever and we all felt very ill by the time we stopped and were taken out into yet another van. After that, there was an even longer journey by road until we finally arrived at our destination which was very much like the place we had left behind in Ireland but bigger with even more dogs.

'Welcome to Battersea Dogs Home,' a nice looking woman said. 'You've all had a long journey and I can tell you are all feeling homesick and seasick so you should all get a good sleep and rest now.'

We certainly agreed with her.

The days went by and lots of people visited us and one by one, all my friends left to go to new families. I was in a dreadful state. My heart was broken and I couldn't eat and I felt very angry at the world. The day Rory found a new family was the last straw for me and I am ashamed to say I bit the woman who came to feed me that morning. I was sorry straight away and cowered in the corner thinking she would hit me. Instead, she came back with another lady and they talked about me in whispers for ages. Then the lady came in and sat down on the floor with me and didn't say a word. I had no idea what to do or think. Eventually she spoke to me: well she spoke to me in my head like some humans can.

'Kenny? It is Kenny isn't it?'

'Yes, how did you know my name?'

'Because I can understand animals and I also understand that you are really unhappy. My name is Donna and I come from Ireland too.'

'Hello Donna, are you going to take me to your home?' I asked hopefully.

She laughed and said, 'If you only knew how many lovely friends I have taken home over the years. If I kept all of them I would need a big house in the country, not my London flat! No, you are coming to live with me for a while and I am going to be your foster mum.'

'That sounds nice,' I said. 'I like you.' I gave her a friendly lick and she gently put out her hand to pat me but I flinched instinctively and backed away because I was understandably so nervous of humans.

'Kenny, I am never going to hurt you, I promise. No one will ever be mean to you again,' she softly said.

I spent the next three months with Donna and she was incredibly kind to me. We went for walks every day and she helped me get over all my fears. I was in a bit of a state really, even after all her kindness to me. I still chewed everything with nerves and jumped when anyone tried to stroke me. However, she patiently taught me some party tricks to help break the ice with strangers and although I thought they were silly, she told me that humans would be charmed by me. After a while, Donna took me with her to her office at Battersea and I stayed in her room in a cage to make me feel secure. I put on a bit of weight but they had to cut off all my long hair because it was all matted and out of condition. I felt more canine than I had for ages and hoped I would soon find someone to take care of me permanently.

It was on a cold and breezy April morning when I looked up to see some people staring at me and looking excited. There were *three men and two girls and I wondered if this was going to be my future family. We were taken into a big room and a warden came in too to introduce us. I really wasn't sure what to do so I offered my paw and hoped they wouldn't judge me too much on my appearance. They seemed to like me! They all wanted to take my paw and they clustered around me and chattered a lot. It was a bit frightening but I studied them all carefully and decided they were kind and caring. Obviously Donna had told them my name so they called to me and were very careful not to all surround me at once. I heard the warden explaining that they would have to come back for another visit if they were serious about taking me. I tried to bark and get their attention to tell them that I really liked them and that seemed to make them laugh.*

It was another seven days before I saw them again but they did come back! Hurray! They took me for a walk in the park and it was great fun but I was so, so frightened that they might not like me and I think my nerves showed a bit because they were discussing me and whether I would fit in. It was so tense. We went back to the home and then I heard the best words I have heard in my life....

'We really like him and would love to take him home with us,' the very tall man said.

'Yes, we would love to give him a home if you think we are suitable,' the kind lady said.

Suitable? They were being inspected too! How funny! Then before I knew it, I was in their car and on my way. Incredible. I had a collar. I had my own lead. I had new feeding bowls. I had a new home. I had a family. I even had a new name, 'Jack' because they felt it was right that I be adopted properly and start all over. It was the best day of my life.

I settled in fast and grew to love each and every member of my new, big family. I was fussed and adored and teased and played with and the house was full of music every day and the very best part of my new life was the fact that the tall man, Les, played lots of instruments and it would remind me of the old days and all my friends and of course, my dear Cathleen who I still miss so very much.

* * * * * * * * * * *

Mrs Tippett cuddled me and told me that was the best story she had ever heard and that she would write it all down for me so people could know all about me. She said I was handsome, brave, loyal, and the best dog she had ever met. I'm not sure about the handsome bit though.....

The Mythical Spring Creature

Hockley Woods sits on a ridge of hills that stretches from Thundersley through Rayleigh and out to Canewdon. You may have noticed that there are churches perched high up in every town along the line of hills and there are interesting historical sites too. From Hadleigh Castle to Rayleigh Mount and Plumberow Mount out to the ancient site of King Canute's camp in Canewdon. There are other lesser known places too: Hambro Hill was an iron-age site and there have been Roman finds in the area as well as Roman roads that still exist today.

You may like to find out more but there is one mysterious legend that has never found its way into any history books because people are not too sure whether they should believe in it or not. It is not a subject that comes up in conversation unless it is in family circles or among close friends because to say you believe it could make strangers think you were a bit bonkers! However, we all know that there are mysteries in the world and some cannot be explained and some are probably not true. This is a tale about a creature that has baffled the people of this part of the world for hundreds of years.

If you live in a house that has a lovely big garden then you may also be lucky enough to have a well too. There are lots of houses in our area that do and there are also lots of houses that have springs.

A spring is where water comes up from underground and makes the ground wet or runs down any slope that may be near. Some of these springs have been dug down to create proper wells and some people have simply pushed long pipes into the spot where the water comes up to make use of the water that is available all the year round, even in times of drought. This source of water has been very valuable to all the people who bought allotments and small amounts of land around this area so they could spend weekends and holidays in the countryside. They would build small wooden dwellings and grow lots of fruit and vegetables.

If you wander around any of the woods in the area, you may suddenly stumble upon old broken brick walls and fruiting apple trees. In the part of Hockley Woods that has now been cut off by farming land there is another area called Grove Woods and there you will find old foundations, garden plants and even a big ditch for waste. In the spring the whole area is full of beautiful blossom from the fruit trees that someone must have planted many decades ago.

It is the network of underground water channels in this part of the world that hides a creature, which is as elusive as the Loch Ness Monster.

One very dark day in winter when it seemed as if the rain would never cease, Lauren and Chris were getting very fed up with being cooped up indoors and were beginning to fight with each other out of boredom. I told them to put on their waterproofs and wellington boots, gloves and scarves.

'Why? It's raining outside,' Lauren moaned.

'Because I am tired of hearing you two squabbling and you need some fresh air,' I replied.

'What can we do in this weather?' Chris enquired.

'You can walk the dogs and bring in some firewood. Then you can have a nice, hot bath.'

'That all sounds boring. I don't want to go outside,' Lauren moaned.

'Well I'm busy cooking and someone needs to do it,' I insisted.

'OK.' They both stomped out.

They were gone quite a long time so I put my head outside the door after about twenty minutes and called them back in. There was no sign of them. I called again and then heard Chris shout back from a long way off that they were coming. When they returned with the very wet dogs I asked them why they had been out so long.

'We met someone, something, some sort of ...... creature,' Chris stammered.

'What are you talking about?' I asked.

'We don't know,' Chris said.

'It was some sort of animal,' Lauren suggested, 'but we have never seen one before.'

'Where did you see it? What did it look like?' I was now intrigued.

'It had wings,' Chris shouted.

'It had scales,' Lauren said excitedly, 'and a beak!'

'What on earth are you two jabbering on about? What was it – a bird?' I asked.

'Not a bird, but a bit like a bird, or like a mini dragon, or a lizard, or a pterodactyl but small.' Lauren said knowledgeably. I was impressed that she knew about prehistoric animals.

'Yes, but it talked to us,' Chris shouted again, getting more and more excited.

'So, let me see if I have got this right. It is like a pterodactyl because it has wings but is also a bit scaly. Are you sure it wasn't just a bedraggled bird – it has been raining a lot?' I asked them reasonably.

'Nooooo mum,' Lauren insisted, 'it's not a wet bird; I would know what that looked like. It's really different..... and .... it .... speaks.'

At this point I realised that I was going to have to go outside in the rain myself or they wouldn't leave me alone. I grabbed my waterproof and wellies and we all went back outside to the garden. The children ran excitedly over to where a large pipe was sunk into the ground with a lid over it to keep the water clean. This was our very own spring and it was very useful for watering the garden in the summer. They looked around the whole area and lifted up the lid and called out but of course, there was nothing there. I put it all down to their ever-fanciful imaginations and thought I really ought to stop telling them made-up bedtime stories.

'I'm sorry children, whatever it was, it must have found somewhere dry to shelter from the rain.' I said, going along with their story.

'Oh Mum, it won't like anywhere dry. It likes wet places like our well and streams and stuff,' Lauren explained patiently.

'Yes, and it travels underground all over the place,' Chris interjected.

'You certainly seem to know a lot about this creature don't you?' I said with amusement. 'Well, I think we had better get back indoors for now and maybe you will see it again soon.'

'Oh!' Lauren and Chris both protested.

I must admit I was surprised – they had never liked playing outside in the wet before! 'Well, all right, just until supper time then.'

I went back indoors and busied myself with the cooking, glancing out of the window every now and again to make sure they were not doing anything too silly. I could tell they were looking very carefully in every bush and plant and wondered what it was that they had seen.

Suddenly I heard Chris cry out and Lauren ran over to where he was crouching low in the huge leaves that hung over the pond. It was a massive plant called Gunnera and you could hide a family of badgers under its huge umbrella-like leaves. I was now very curious but unfortunately the chips were nearly done and it really was time for their dinner. I called out of the back door for them to come in.

I could see a lot of hand gestures and excited behaviour and then they ran down to the back door, threw off their wet clothes and washed their hands. All this time, they were looking at each other with the biggest grins you have ever seen. They sat down at the table and started their meal without saying a word. If this was designed to make me curious – it certainly worked.

'Well?' I asked.

'What Mum?' Lauren replied, smiling like the cat that got the cream.

'Don't be cheeky Lauren. Did you find your little friend again?'

Chris could not stop smiling like someone who has just found a hidden treasure and been told they could keep it all.

'Yes, we did, and his name is Xerosophiles – pronounced zero, soffi, leez.' Lauren announced proudly.

'He said we can just call him Xero,' Chris joined in. 'Apparently there are lots more like him, but grown-ups pretend they don't exist!'

'And his name is a joke because he said something about xero meaning dry but he has to stay wet.'

'He said they like it around here because there are lots of places where there is water underground.'

'Goodness, it sounds like you have been having a geography lesson! Where did you learn all this stuff?' I asked, completely confounded by this barrage of information. I am sure they could never have made up all these strange names and facts. Even I had never heard of zero or xero, however it should be spelt, being a word that means dry. I decided to test them on this to see how it was spelt and then I would go and look it up.

'So, how does your friend spell his name then?' I challenged them.

'X E R O S O P H I L E S,' Chris proclaimed proudly. He always loved big, long words because he read so much.

'Oh,' was all I could say, completely dumbfounded. 'It starts with X then?'

'Yes,' they chorused.

'Well, I need to look this up then,' I said and went out to my bookshelf for a dictionary. Lo and behold, there was something that seemed familiar. I found the word "xerophiles" being some kind of mould that needed very dry conditions – so I understood why the creature's name was a joke, if indeed, he needed wet conditions to survive. The mystery deepened.

'Hmm, I'm really not sure about this and whether you are playing a trick on me. I think you had better tell me if you ever see this chap again and hopefully I will be able to see it with my own eyes. Seeing is believing.'

The children smiled at me and looked up with their best "you can really believe us" expressions.

'Yes, Mum. We'll call you next time,' Lauren said.

The months went by and I must admit I did forget about the children's game that day and they didn't talk about it either. However, I was visiting a friend in Rayleigh on a lovely, warm, early spring day and we sat outside to drink our tea. My friend had a very large well at the bottom of her garden that was quite a beautiful, brick-built construction with a roof and a proper bucket to lower into the water. It made our pipe and lid in the ground look very poor indeed. I mentioned the well to her and asked if it still had water in the summer. She replied that it always had water even in drought conditions and that everyone in her street had a well at the bottom of their gardens. I was really surprised and wondered why the area had so many. She seemed quite knowledgeable, having lived in Rayleigh all her life, and told me that there were so many springs in the area and there was even a road named after them, Spring Gardens!

She then went on with a knowing smile to say, 'There is a legend in Rayleigh about a mythical spring creature that travels underground between all the houses and pops out in their wells!'

Well, you could have knocked me down with a feather! I was so surprised. However, I did not tell her about the children's story because I honestly felt a little foolish. Instead, I laughed and remarked on how folklore lives on even in the twenty first century!

'Yes, I am sure it is just as elusive as the Loch Ness Monster,' my friend replied.

We talked a little more about whether anyone she knew had ever seen anything but apparently nobody had for decades and now it was just the stuff of legend. My friend then told me about the disappearance of so many ponds and rivers in the area in the last hundred years or more. There used to be a pond right by the large roundabout known as Rayleigh Weir and of course that made sense because a weir is a small barrier to keep water in. There was also a pond on the site where the recycling station exists now in Castle Road in Rayleigh and the water that fed that pond was used in the local brewery back in the nineteenth century.

I then remembered the Hockley Spa that people came from far and wide to visit. The water that rose up from the springs in Hockley was supposed to be very good for you and a beautiful building was erected for people to come and bathe and drink the local water. The spa closed many years ago and most people have forgotten about it. It is only the names that remind us of what used to be before the railway came and all the houses were built in the area.

Despite all this talk of springs, ponds and streams, I was all set to completely dismiss the whole idea of legendary animals but I knew my children and I knew they were not the sort of people to make up such a story and, besides, where would they have heard about it anyway? I decided not to mention anything to them but just bided my time until something else happened.

August soon came but it was not the best of summer holidays that year. There were two extremely hot days when the temperature rose to almost thirty degrees and then there was a huge thunderstorm in the middle of the afternoon on the second day that flooded the lawn in seconds. There were hailstones as big as peas; thunderclaps that echoed for ages and lightning that sent me running around the house to unplug all the television aerials! As the storm faded I ran outside to rescue my washing and I asked the children to come and help. Within a few minutes, the sun came out and the temperature started to climb again. I decided to leave the washing out with a glance at the sky to see if there were any more thundery clouds around.

Suddenly, Chris cried out. 'He's here; he's back, quick come and see!'

'Who? What? What are you talking about? Lauren replied.

'It's Xero!' Chris shouted with joy.

I didn't know what to do. Should I follow my children or should I pretend to be very adult and disinterested?

I eventually walked over as casually as I could to where the children were crouching on the ground near our well.

What I saw defies description. I honestly could not believe my own eyes. There by the well was the weirdest creature I have ever seen, even on some of those underwater nature programmes on the television. It stood about thirty centimeters tall with a beak nearly the same size. In fact, it looked so top heavy I was amazed it didn't topple forward. Luckily it had very large webbed feet to keep its balance. I also realised that this strange animal had folded up its wings so when they were fully outstretched they must have measured about ninety centimeters across.

His eyes were very large and dark - so dark you could hardly see his round pupils and just below his eyes were intriguing nostrils that had a membrane that you could see moving in and out as he breathed. They looked a bit like gills on a fish but round rather than vertical flaps.

I hardly had time to take all this in before I understood that it was communicating with Lauren and Chris. It sounded like a parrot and it was quite hard to understand.

Bit by bit, I started to make out what it was saying. Lauren turned to me excitedly and said, 'I told you Mum. Xero has been away exploring and meeting his friends. He says one of his main underground passages has been dug up to make room for a new road so he had to find another way round. In the end he had to go over-ground at night time which he says is really dangerous.'

Chris then explained, 'Xero looks a bit like a heron when he flies and sometimes people do see him but just assume that is what he is.'

I knelt down on the grass and looked very closely at the wonderful new animal we had discovered.

'I'm pleased to meet you,' I found myself saying, feeling very foolish.

'And you too,' Xero replied in a croaky, squeaky sort of voice.

'Where do you come from?' I asked.

'Here, of course!' he replied.

'Yes, but what are you? Why haven't we seen you before?'

'I was hiding,' Xero said.

'Hiding from humans?' I asked, feeling sure this would be true.

'Hiding from everything,' he said enigmatically.

'Oh. Are you the only one of your kind?'

'No Mum, we told you - there are more of them,' Lauren explained patiently.

'There are lots of us, all around this area. Many thousands of years ago there used to be even more of us and we were much bigger then,' Xero said proudly.

'Are you some kind of dinosaur?' I suggested.

'Din-o-saur. Hmm, I have heard that word before. I don't know what you call us but in the days before human beings lived here, there were lots of very big creatures and food was plentiful. Now, we are all very small because the planet is so overpopulated and we are running out of things to eat. Some of those gigantic creatures disappeared millions of years ago and some just a few hundred years ago. My friends and I are probably the last of our kind.'

'Goodness me, so you must be related to the huge flying creatures from prehistoric times that used to live in this part of the world. Well I never!' I was truly taken aback and still not quite believing this bizarre encounter.

We heard a rumble of thunder in the distance and the temperature was rising again.

'So do you live underground now?' I asked him.

'Yes, we all do. It's much safer and we can travel around quite easily in the underground rivers and channels. Sometimes we use the streams and rivers around here – there are so many of them – and no one can see us. We have to be a bit more careful though because of boats and fishermen.'

'That sounds so dangerous. I hope you never get caught,' Chris said.

Xero laughed and said, 'Yes, it would be quite frightening to catch us wouldn't it? Imagine the fisherman's face if he pulled one of us out of the water. Don't worry, we are so quick and it's so easy to break a fishing line with our lovely sharp beaks.'

'Do you eat fish?' Lauren asked.

'Oh yes, fish and shrimp but not toads – they're poisonous!'

'Goodness me, I really cannot believe all this. Why have you been friendly with my children?' I asked Xero.

'Because they can keep a secret and because they care about animals. That's very unusual nowadays. Please can I ask you not to tell anyone else? If anyone hears about us, I know they will try and find us and kill us. I know some have been caught and taken to places where they keep them locked up while they try to find out more about us but no one ever comes back. You must promise. You really must.'

'We all promise don't we?' I said solemnly, looking at the children.

'Yes, we promise. We really do.' Lauren and Chris answered.

'I hope to see you again one day. Don't forget me,' Xero announced as he prepared to dive down our well.

'Oh don't go,' Lauren called.

'Please stay a bit longer,' Chris begged.

'I think Xero will come back, won't you?' I smiled at him.

'Yes, one day, but I must go before any more rain comes because it's getting quite flooded and it means swimming upstream!' Xero laughed.

'We really hope to see you again. It has been a real honour to meet you,' I whispered, hardly daring to believe this was all true.

Before you could blink an eye, Xero had dived, beak first, into our well and there was not even a ripple to show where he had been. We all felt very sad and sorry for ourselves. The rain had started again and the thunder sounded closer. We went back indoors and sat in the kitchen not knowing what to do or say.

'We must keep this a secret,' I urged the children, 'Nobody would believe us anyway. Please promise me.'

'Yes. We already promised Xero before you saw him today. We didn't think he would let you see him,' Lauren said forlornly.

'I hope he comes back soon,' Chris sniffed.

'Can we tell Dad?' Lauren asked.

'Of course you can. I'm sure it will be all right if we just keep it to the family but we will have trouble convincing them that we are telling the truth. After all, if you didn't actually see Xero, you really wouldn't believe he existed would you?' I replied.

'He is so amazing though, isn't he,' Lauren remarked.

'Yes, probably the most amazing thing I have seen in my life,' I answered.

Well, Xero did come back. He did not appear very often but I never saw him again. The children used to tell me when he had been visiting but said he seemed very nervous because more and more roads and houses were being built in the area. He said he and all his friends had to travel by night and sometimes, even fly, which was exceedingly risky. Lauren and Chris were very worried that soon, none of these creatures would be left like so many endangered species. However, at least we were among the very few lucky people to encounter the mythical spring creature and that was a privilege indeed.

 Now I've shared the secret with you, dear reader, make sure you keep it too won't you?

* * * * * * * * * * * *

Sometimes, as I drive to work in the early mornings, I am lucky enough to see a heron. It rises up into the air and soars majestically over the fields that line the busy road before swooping down to another small stream. Sometimes, in the early morning light, I think there is something odd about it. It may be a trick of the light but the beak looks far too long for a heron.....

Parson's Snipe

There is an area of Hockley Woods that few people go to because it seems to be quite a lonely place that extends out into farmland with no way back other than the way you came.

In the spring, this area is completely covered in bluebells and their wonderful fragrance fills the air. I am glad it is so quiet because it means the flowers are left unspoiled or damaged by thoughtless visitors.

Parson's Snipe is a reminder of just how large the forest used to be. Before we needed so much land for farming, the woodland stretched for acre upon acre but over the centuries it has slowly been reduced in size. Beyond this small jetty of trees there used to be an area called Splash Wood that led to another area that still exists called Dark Wood. Other smaller woods have been cut off from the main forest and each has their own personality but our story is all about this secret corner.

I should maybe mention that I am retelling events that happened to my eldest daughter Faye. You may remember that she is a bit older than Lauren and Chris and when she was old enough and at secondary school, I let her take the dogs out for walks to help me when I was busy.

When Faye was still at junior school we explored much of the woodland together and loved this area in the spring but also in the autumn when the leaves started to change colour. One particular September afternoon we were out together on the way back from school and stopped off to take some photographs.

We walked out of the trees into the late afternoon sunshine and saw the most amazing sight. Just on the edge of the recently cleared wheat field, we saw a very alien looking object. This was the first and only time we encountered a puffball mushroom. It was huge, the size of a football and absolutely, perfectly white. I asked Faye to crouch down next to the mushroom for a photograph and it made her look quite small! Mind you, Faye was very petite and even though she was in her last year of junior school she was probably the smallest girl in her class! We felt really special to have seen a puffball mushroom because they are quite rare and often get damaged very quickly.

Faye never forgot the unusual mushroom and in her mind, she associated the encounter with this part of the woods. It became one of her favourite places to go when she went running or walking the dogs.

Now, I am sure you think adventures do not happen to older people but if you are the sort of person that loves nature and likes to be outdoors, then you will understand how much there is to see and learn about all around us. Faye loved being in the countryside and you may remember that she often found injured birds or animals to take home and nurture back to health. Sometimes I would go into her room and be surprised by some unusual creatures. Once it was a slow worm and another time a baby grass snake that was born very late when the first frosts arrived. She kept gerbils and mice for many years and absolutely adored our ginger tomcat called Humbug.

The family was always in awe of Faye when we visited Greenwich Park in London because she was able to just crouch near the trees and squirrels and pigeons would come to her to be fed from her hand. Lauren and Chris used to stand open-mouthed as these shy animals were more than happy to sit on her shoulder or arm while she stroked them. Admittedly, they were tamer than their wilder cousins but even so, no one else seemed to have Faye's connection with animals.

It is therefore no surprise at all to learn that Faye was a very well-known visitor in Hockley Woods. She always took the same path down from the house, over the small bridge and onto the boundary walk. She then took a lesser-known route straight across the central path in the direction of a school that backed onto the woodland. This was a favourite path for all the family and the dogs because it involved climbing over fallen trees from the hurricane of 1987 and passed our 'wishing tree'. This was a lovely beech tree that had a completely straight trunk except for three noticeable rings that grew out from the trunk close to each other and low enough for us to reach with our hands. We would all put our hands on the rings and wish hard for something that was on our minds. From the wishing tree, the path turns towards the ponds on the far side of the woods where it is sandy and quite open and then, turning uphill, is the path out towards Eastwood and, of course, Parson's Snipe.

On a particular spring day when it was suddenly very warm, Faye asked if she could take Pebble and Merlin out for a run. She was already in her trainers and obviously itching to get out so I naturally said yes but not to be too long. She opened the back door and the dogs needed no encouragement to bound out in front of her and bark noisily as they all set off. I knew where she would be and imagined how lovely the woods would be today with their fresh green leaves.

Hockley Woods in springtime is wonderful. The forest floor is covered with wood anenomes, yellow archangel, bluebells and rare species like cow wheat. The leaves on the trees are bright with hope and many are covered in blossom. You just know that the better the spring, the more likely it is that there will be a fantastic harvest of chestnuts, blackberries and sloe berries in the autumn.

Faye soon reached the top of the hill and slowed down for a rest and to let the dogs have a breather. They were very happy to lap up water from some puddles and flop down in the sun that filtered down through the treetops. From this high vantage point you could see all the way to Southend-on-Sea, Eastwood, Rayleigh and Rochford across the fields.

She then walked slowly over to Parson's Snipe treading very carefully to avoid crushing all the wild flowers. The softest of breezes was blowing and the silken threads of spider trails were moving slowly to and fro between the trees. Faye knew that she was the first person to walk through there that day because none of the threads had been broken.

The shafts of sunlight were reflecting off millions of tiny specks of pollen that rose from all the flowers and it felt like walking through a cathedral with beautiful stained glass windows pouring colour all around. Suddenly a tiny furry animal sped across her path and she laughed to see a little weasel scurrying through last year's fallen leaves. Luckily neither Merlin nor Pebble had seen it as they were far too busy sniffing around some trees further ahead. She started humming the tune to 'Pop Goes the Weasel' to herself but then thought better of it because she knew she would need to stay very quiet if she was going to see any more wildlife.

Faye reached the very heart of the small copse where the trees were thin and flowers carpeted the floor. This was the place to stop and have a drink and rest awhile. She lay back and gazed up at the sky and the dogs lay beside her with their tongues hanging out. Slowly, they all drifted off to sleep in the warm sunshine.

As time slowly passed, they were all unaware of a very special event that was taking place in the old, dry leaves they were resting on. Some of these leaves were quite curled up and inside them a small miracle was taking place. One by one, the leaves began to stir and you would be forgiven for thinking they were coming alive! However, each curled up leaf contained the beginnings of a butterfly and slowly but surely they were emerging into the glorious spring day ready to open their wings for the very first time. Inside each leaf was a protective case called a chrysalis which is the home that a caterpillar makes to keep it warm in the winter while it changes into an amazing butterfly the next spring or summer.

The butterflies were a bit wobbly on their legs while they balanced on a leaf or twig and dried their wings. They were also impatient to try them out but each of them was waiting to get warm so that they could fly well. They were all the same kind of butterfly that is very rare and protected in our country.

When Faye woke up, she could not believe what had happened. She was completely surrounded by wonderful floating clouds of orange, white and brown wings. She kept really still and stroked the dogs to keep them as quiet as possible. Some of the butterflies landed on her and she was able to see them close up. This was the closest she had ever been to one and she knew she was really lucky. She could see their tiny eyes peering at her and their antennae that constantly moved as they detected the smells in the air. Every now and then, a tiny tongue came out tasting her skin and clothing to see if she was food or not! Their wings were slightly hairy up close and the colours were striking but also very good camouflage in the brown leaves and flowers.

If you were walking through the woods that day, you would not have been able to see Faye or the dogs because they were completely submerged under a host of bright, beautiful, breathtaking butterflies in the brilliant midday sunshine. The Heath Fritillary butterflies filled the air and were ready to make the most of the English summer.

She was incredibly blessed to see such an event and it added to the fairy-like quality of Parson's Snipe. For Faye, this was a place she knew she would always return to and she could not wait to come back and tell me about what had happened.

Many years later, I was cycling with my husband along the fields above Grove Woods and we decided to continue with our ride by doing our favourite circular route out along the newly established park and pathways called Cherry Orchard Way. We stopped by the two large ponds to watch all the local dogs swimming and fetching sticks in the cool water and remarked how lucky we were to have such a beautiful area right on our doorstep. I asked if he felt like climbing up the hill to Gusted Hall Lane via Parson's Snipe and he agreed.

After a bit of puffing and panting (we were not as young as we used to be) we arrived at the top of the hill to be rewarded by a clear view all the way to Canewdon, the old Rochford hospital tower, out to sea and the Maplin Sands, the amazing new university building on Southend sea front and then round to

Green Lane in Eastwood and finally the woods which obscured the view over to Rayleigh Mount with the church and windmill.

When we reached the edge of Parson's Snipe we were amazed to see hundreds of strange flying insects. At first we thought they were butterflies but on closer inspection we saw they were quite exotic looking and thought they might be a visitor from abroad. That sometimes happens in hot summers. We remembered seeing humming bird moths in one of the hottest summers on record when the temperature reached over 33 degrees and even over 37 degrees during one incredible week. This moth had the longest antennae you have ever seen as well as very distinctive markings on its wings. They were dancing in and out of the beech trees in a crowd all along the edges of the fields. They were all flying up and up and then dropping back down to the leaves they started on, almost as though their antennae were weighing them down! There were so many of them as far as you could see but only where the sun was shining. As soon as you went further into the trees, there were none to be seen. They obviously enjoyed sunbathing!

We had never seen anything like it but we now know that it is called a Fairy Moth and I think it is the most fitting name for a moth that lives in this part of Hockley Woods because it really is full of magic and surprises.

All those years ago when I found out I was going to have my first child I remember a dream I had about having a little girl called Faye. I now know that she could not have had a better name for a special person who seems to have such a connection with little creatures. Faye means fairy – I wonder if she becomes one when I'm not looking!